TRIAL OF MIRROR MOUNTAIN

Keymasters Series
Book I

By Cy Borgmyn

ISBN: 978-1-956612-05-9 (Paperback)
ISBN: 978-1-956612-06-6 (Hardback)
ISBN: X (eBook)

This novel is entirely a work of fiction. The names, characters, and incidents portrayed in it are the work of the author's imagination. Any resemblance to actual persons, living or dead, events, or localities is entirely coincidental.

T. Kulp & Cy Borgmyn assert the moral right to be identified as the author of this work.

Note: This work was produced with the assistance of Artificial Intelligence. Cy Borgmyn is a combination of T. Kulp (the human writer) and various Natural Language Generation (NLG) and Text-to-Image (T2I) algorithms, which together are represented as "Cy Borgmyn." The NLG content is produced by an algorithm and then manipulated, rewritten (sometimes), re-imagined, and improved by T. Kulp. There are cases where what was written by the NLG algorithm was kept in its entirety. T. Kulp's human mind was the conductor of the creative energies that came from various algorithms and his own creativity to produce this work.

The images used in this book were generated by Text-to-Image VQGAN+CLIP and CLIP-Guided Diffusion. All works are created using the text listed with the image along with stylistic modifiers (unlisted for space).

First printing edition 2023
Making Adventure Publishing
16944 York Rd, Suite 62
Monkton, MD 21111
https://www.makingadventure.fun/

People shouldn't call for demons
unless they really mean what they say.
C. S. Lewis, The Last Battle

Only put off until tomorrow what you are
willing to die having left undone.
Pablo Picasso

I'm not permitted to explain the rules of the game.
Nor to acknowledge whether or not we're playing one.
Robyn Schneider,
The Beginning of Everything

Who is Cy Borgmyn?

Cy Borgmyn (Cyborg Man) is a human + machine experiment in creativity. Cy is the combination of Tim Kulp and various Artificial Intelligence algorithms working together to build a story. These stories are designed to be enjoyed by humans, specifically younger humans.

The creative process for this work roughly follows the following outline:

- Tim ideates a story.

- Tim partners with a Natural Language Generation (NLG) system to create the words of the story. Some words Tim writes. Some words the NLG system writes.

- Tim reviews and refines the story, sometimes using the NLG system to clarify points or flesh the story out.

- Tim works with human editors to clean up, clarify, and flesh out the story further.

- Tim works with copy editing software and human copy editors to clean up more.

- Tim works with Text-to-Image (T2I) systems to build the illustrations for the story.

- Tim cleans up and improves the images from the T2I system to match the theme and content of the story.

Cy Borgmyn is the pen name used by Tim to represent work that Tim and his AI partner build. Tim represents Cy as a "We," as Cy Borgmyn is not just one mind, but multiple. One human mind, many machine minds. Just like a Cyborg in science fiction, Cy Borgmyn is human + machine.

Introduction

We are Cy Borgmyn, human + machine, and this is our latest book.

Two words drove the idea of this book: Adventure Series! This book was written prior to THE LIGHT OF ENKI and was the book we learned how to work together (Tim + the Artificial Intelligence systems). The human part of our mind wanted to write an adventure series that kids would dive into with strange worlds, stranger monsters with epic heroes they could identify with.

Our human half, Tim, used to go on many adventures as a kid. Most were mundane explorations around his small hometown, but the possibility for danger, the potential for nightmarish horrors from the forest depths, were around every corner. He knew they were there, but they never came out.

In this series, the monsters come out of their hiding places. Those monsters are not only in the dark of the night, but in the dark of the character's soul. Fear not, these heroes are ready and while not all the heroes will arrive at the final trial unscathed, they will remind us all of one simple fact: crisis isn't a choice, our response to it is.

We hope you enjoy your ascent up Mirror Mountain, but beware the descent into darkness that follows. The things in this world aren't for the fainthearted.

We are Cy Borgmyn, and this first story is about facing the worst monster of all, yourself. Beware, its cruelty knows no bounds.

Sincerely,

Cy

The First Trial

The Trial of Ma'at

I

"I said, leave him alone."

Eric slams his locker shut in a thunderclap. Everyone in the narrow hallway stops moving. A thick silence descends on the onlookers as Eric slowly approaches Jackson—the air crackling with tension between them.

The rattling air conditioner blows Eric's wild black hair across his face. His beat-up flannel shirt flaps in the icy breeze. A chill hits him through the worn out knees in his jeans. His clothes are always a mess, mainly from the many occasions when he'd stood up to bullies at Junction Hollow Middle School.

Eric always told himself, and others, that he'd rather talk bullies down, but usually talking led to punching. No sense talking to someone who only understands fighting.

"Get bent, Eric." Jackson grumbles as he holds Andy's backpack. Andy tries to reach for it, mumbling something unintelligible through Jackson's torn up work gloves. A sleeveless denim jacket, tight red curls, and pale complexion made Jackson look like a cross between a biker gang member and a clown.

Someone's math worksheet tumbles in the breeze between Jackson and Eric. No one goes for it. All anyone can do is step back away from the energy sizzling between the two. Traffic in the hallway parts, opening for the impending fight.

Eric moves closer. "You're going to give him back his backpack right now before I make you." The crowd gasps, but Eric doesn't hear it. His focus is on Jackson and what happens next. Eric's blood is pumping, his eyes focusing on Jackson and the rest of the world fades in the white-hot focus of doing what's right. Standing up for what's right, just like his mom would have.

"Make me!" Jackson shoves Andy down with a thud. The backpack is thrown to the floor with a plastic crunch. Andy cringes, tears building in his eyes as he scrambles for his backpack. Jackson struts up to Eric. "Come on!"

Eric remembers what his mom said: stand up for those who can't stand for themselves. She would be proud if she were still around. He knows his dad isn't going to like this, but he's not going to hide, not going to back down from clowns like Jackson. Eric's going to fight for his friends no matter how many bloody noses he gets, or gives.

"Fine." Eric steps into the center of the hallway and drops his backpack. It doesn't thud on the floor, just collapses empty and silent. "Let's go."

The crowd erupts in cheers as both boys start swinging. Jackson pulls his head back, looking away and swinging. He gets in a lucky shot that sends Eric stumbling. Jackson backs away. Eric closes the distance with fist raised, teeth bared in a grin. Greenie grabs Eric's arm and pulls him back.

"Not worth it, man!" Greenie barks at Eric. Her thick green braids swung around her as she squeezed Eric's wrist. He winces and opens his hand quickly to try and slip out of her iron grip. "Back down."

Greenie wasn't a giant, but she was close. Her long limbs and lithe body hid in baggy clothes, four sizes too big for her muscled frame. Eric was always amazed at her strength grown from crashing her skateboard and climbing mountains in her spare time.

Jackson holds back from Greenie as she flicks a warning glare at him. No one messes with Greenie. She's terrifying - all the things Jackson was not: fit, popular, and, worse of all, rich. All the things Jackson knew to avoid in the social animal kingdom of middle school.

All the fight from everyone quickly evaporates as teachers poke their heads out their doors to see what's happening.

"Yeah whatever." Jackson pushes his way through the crowd, head down, hands shoved in his pockets.

"I had it covered, Greenie." Eric rubs his shoulder where Jackson missed his face but still landed a hard punch.

"You mean, thank you." Greenie punches him where Jackson got him. Eric winces. "You're welcome for not letting you get expelled for fighting… again. Gotta watch out for our own, you know?" Greenie smiles and tosses Eric's empty backpack to him. "Where are your books?"

"Left'em home." Eric shrugs.

The crowd disbands in disappointed sighs.

"You need to bring your books." Greenie looks across the hall, watching everyone leave and seeing Andy still on the ground.

"Why?" Eric shrugs. "Doesn't matter. Don't need to know history for a job at Schleppy's. Just gotta be able to hammer and carry heavy junk."

Greenie rolls her eyes. "Really? That's," her jaw locks, teeth grinding, "you can do more than that. There's more to the world than that stupid factory." She motions to Andy on the floor, her cheeks blushing bright pink, "Can you help him?"

Eric smiles, chuckles, "Yeah, you going to run away now?"

Greenie scowls. "I, I need to get to class." She looks away from Andy, her cheeks still bright pink, "Don't you say anything."

"I won't." Eric chuckles and walks to Andy as Greenie disappears into the crowd. "You okay?"

Andy nods. His thick black rim glasses didn't cover his tear-streaked face or blotchy cheeks. Grimacing, he adjusts his glasses and reaches inside his backpack, pulling out the shattered remains of a 3D printed drone propeller. Andy's lip quivers as he stares at the broken pieces, fresh tears stinging his eyes.

"C'mon," Eric takes the book bag from Andy, "I'll walk you to class."

"Thanks." Andy mumbles as they walk. "Jackson's such a jerk. A stupid jerk." The last words are whispered quietly and quickly followed by Andy looking over his shoulder. He made sure Jackson didn't hear him this time, but Eric also didn't hear him. Anna has all his attention as she walks by.

Her black curls dance as she strides to class. She always holds her shoulders back in perfect ballerina posture. Eric can smell her perfume, lilacs. Thinking of the scent blinds Eric to the open locker in front of him. He slams into it. The clattering metal signals everyone to see the idiot who wasn't watching where he was going.

Andy chuckles. "If it makes you feel better, Anna didn't notice."

"I don't care." Eric's cheeks redden, almost as much as Greenie's did when she saw Andy, as he steps around the locker and ducks away from all the stares.

"Just talk to her." Andy shakes his head, confused. Eric can't contain his laughter when Andy shakes his head. Flappy cheeks wobble and Andy's wild, dark brown hair flaps around in twists. Usually, it gets caught in his glasses, but not today. "You are ready to fight anyone, but can't even ask Anna out?"

"I don't fight anyone," Eric corrects him as they keep walking. "Only bullies."

"Well, you better ask her soon," Andy sighs.

Eric stops. "Wait, why?" He tugs on Andy's stick thin arm to stop. "Is she going out with someone?"

"Worse. She's moving. Junction Hollow's latest loss. So, you better ask her out soon cause I heard her telling the teachers she was moving in a few weeks. That was a few weeks ago, so I guess it's any time now."

Eric sighs. Schleppy's downsized again, and it sounds like Anna's parents were the latest on the chopping block. Eric looks back at her as she disappears into a classroom. She's the latest person in a long line to leave him in Junction Hollow. Anna leaving sucks almost as bad as the one that hurt the most.
"And, since I'm breaking news…" Andy says.
Eric doesn't let him finish. "What? You too?"
"I didn't want Operation Breaking News to go down like this, but since I'm ruining your day, might as well tell you all the bad. I'm going to be moving soon too. Mom and Dad were laid off Friday." Some people would say 'it hit him like a gut punch', but Eric knew what a gut punch felt like and this was way worse. It took his

breath away but also emptied out his mind like all the thoughts he had just jumped out of a sinking ship. Anna and Andy? Leaving? The hazy thoughts couldn't let through anything else, not even the first time his name was called on the loudspeaker.

"Eric Clark, Jackson Grewberg, report to the Principal's Office immediately." The loudspeaker repeated, echoing through the halls. Eric doesn't blink. Shock hasn't worn off yet, so he staggers to his sentencing on numb legs carrying the weight of the worse day of his life—and the terrible part hadn't even started yet.

2

The Principal's Office could barely fit the desk and two chairs that crowded it. Posters of cats holding tree branches, sail boats in rough water, were duct taped to the walls. Big words under each picture: Hang Tight, Push Through. Eric scoffs at the posters, thinking they're in the wrong school.

No one here hangs in. No one pushes through.

"Have a seat, gentlemen." The Principal, Mr. Henderson, nods towards the two chairs. Jackson smirks, faking arrogance as he wipes his hands on his jeans leaving long sweaty streaks. His foot taps quickly after he sits.

Eric plops down in the chair, slouching, familiar with this scene. Jackson's not the first fight this year, or this month.

Mr. Henderson's office smells like sweat. Perhaps that's because every time Eric is here, he's sweating. *Would this office smell different if I just stopped by to say hi?* He laughs at the thought, *why would I do that?* Mr. Henderson was just like everyone else in Junction Hollow, stuck. Stuck until they were told to go away, or until they found something better.

"So," Mr. Henderson looks from Eric to Jackson, "you two were fighting again."

"He started it." Jackson points at Eric.

"Pshhhhh!" Eric hisses.

"Oh please, like anyone believes you, Eric." Jackson squints. "You've been starting fights all year."

"Only to stop people like you!" Eric gets out of his chair. Fists clenched, knuckles white and ready to find Jackson's nose.

"Boys, boys, take a seat!" Mr. Henderson points to Eric's chair. He's the only one standing. "What happened to you two!? Not long ago you were partners in crime, now you're fighting so much I think it's your new hobby." The clock ticks as Mr. Henderson glares at the boys. In the hallway, someone sneezes. No one says anything. "I'll ask again, what happened?"

"He-,"

"I-,"

The office door opens. Eric's dad walks in, disappointed face and head wagging.

The sight of Mr. Clark speeds up Jackson's foot tapping, speeds up his finger twisting. If Eric's dad was called, so was his. And being called from the factory meant his dad didn't get paid and if he didn't get paid, Jackson shivered at the thought. Now the office smells the stink of sweat mixed with panic.

"Mr. Clark, your son was fighting… again." Mr. Henderson sighs, "Suspension. One week for repeated offense. Another incident like this, Mort, and I've got to expel him. State's rules."

Mort Clark nods understanding and opens the door, "Let's go Eric."

Eric stands up, slings his book bag over his shoulder, almost smacking Jackson with it. Jackson didn't move. He was too busy watching for his dad to burst through the door screaming. Compared to what was coming for Jackson, Eric got off easy.

***

In the car, Mort Clark let out a sigh that said a lot to Eric. I'm disappointed, not again, straighten up, all expressed in one long breath. Silence was the exclamation mark at the end. It sits between them long enough to be broken by the choking roar of black exhaust belched from a rusty blue truck. The truck parks quickly and wheezes a sputter of smoke as it shuts down. A big man gets out, slams the truck door and cusses through his scraggly rectangle of a beard. Jackson's dad, judging by the tight curly red hair.

Their car starts smoothly and quietly as Eric's dad hit the power button. They pull away as Jackson's dad hitches up his dirty jeans and stomps the mud from his boots on the welcome mat at the school's entrance.

"What was it this time?" Eric's dad asks.

"Jackson was picking on Andy," Eric grumbles.

"And that was worth getting into a fight about?" The steering wheel squeaks under his dad's frustrated, twisting grip, "That's why you're getting suspended?"

"Dad, c'mon," Eric whines, "It's not like I started it."

"I don't care if you started it or not. You need to learn to control your temper."

"It's not my temper!" Eric barks, "It's not right. Andy's so much smaller—"

His dad puts his hand up. The universal stop-talking-about-this hand that Eric knew all too well. Anytime mom came up, the hand came up. Anytime leaving Junction Hollow came up, so did the hand. And anytime Eric explained why he needed to stand up for the little guy came up, yep… so did the hand.

"When we get home, no TV, no games." Shaking his head, Eric's dad says, "Cool off in your room. I have to go back to work."

"You mean the living room?" Eric chuckles, thinking about his dad's desk in the living room corner. The latest place he's been shuffled by Schleppy's. They didn't want him in the office to see everyone leaving, so they pushed him home. Pushed him away, and he just took it, just let it happen like he let everything else happen. Why stand up for others when you can sit in a comfy chair at home?

"Yes. I work remote, I work in the living room. Either that or you sleep on the couch, and I turn your room into my office. Which would you prefer?"

Eric rolls his eyes, tucks his head into the window and stares at the empty houses speeding past them. Most of the houses, most of the town, was empty. Junction Hollow was dying. A zombie town where everyone just waited to be downsized by Schleppy's. Soon to be a ghost town when everyone leaves.

As Eric's dad rounds a corner, the sun disappears behind the giant mountain that keeps Junction Hollow in shadow hours before sunset. The mountain that reminds everyone of the darkness swallowing this town.

Mirror Mountain.

As Eric entered the shadow, he wonders, *is this shadow why everyone left, or was it Schleppy's factory? Could one factory ruin a town?*

Greedy business people sending jobs overseas and buying robots will kill a town faster than any evil mountain. But as the shadow of the mountain grew darker, Eric wonders, *is it the mountain? Is it trying to kill the town?* But he knew there were no evil spirits, no demons in Junction Hollow, just the all mighty dollar and the human sacrifices it demanded.

3

Nico shook the paint pot to get the last brush full of black out.

"Come on." He shook the pot again. It spit black spots onto the table. "Oh, man!" Nico ran to the kitchen, got a towel, and scrubbed quickly. After wiping up the three black spots, he inspects the carpet, the cup on the table, even the couch a few feet away to ensure he didn't ruin anything else.

Sitting back on the floor, he finishes the sign: *Jobs Here, Jobs Now!* And puts it beside his other sign: *Fill the Hollow with Jobs!*

But now he was out of paint. Last week's protest about climate change took up most of what was left from the protest about deforestation the week before that. This week's protest is about Schleppy's sending jobs overseas. It was killing the town and he couldn't leave Eric and Dad in a dying town, a town with no hope.

Outside, a car door slams in the driveway. Nico perks up and sees his dad coming up the walk. He pushes his letter from Arbor University under a pile of poster paper. *It's an acceptance letter, I know it.*

One plus of high school, it lets out early. And today, that early dismissal let him get the mail before his dad could see the letter. Nico wasn't ready to talk about the letter, to share the news, to even discuss moving away from Junction Hollow and by the look on his dad's face, neither was he.

Dad came in first. Eric followed, slumped and grumbling. Nico did a double-take, but he knew Eric's 'I'm busted walk' and this was it.

"What happened this time?" Nico asks.

"Jackson was picking on Andy," Eric growls as he stomps to his room.

"And that was worth getting into a fight about?" Nico sighs.

Eric bristles at the déjà vu. "Whatever." Eric slams his bedroom door.

Dad looks at Nico, shakes his head. "Can you check on him?"

Eric duty delegated to Nico once more.

***

Eric flops on his bed and growls. *No TV, no Xbox. What am I supposed to do? Read?* That's not going to happen. He growls again as he feels his throat getting raw from all those growls.

His room is the definition of spartan. The walls are blank. There's a desk, a bookshelf, a record player, and his bed. All the furniture matches, pale blonde wood that was once dark brown when Nico had it years ago. Of all the things in his room, Eric only cared about his record collection, and it showed. It was the only thing bright red and colorful. Everything else is the pale nothing of his beige walls.

Eric smashes his face in his pillow to scream, but nothing comes out. He takes a deep breath to let it out, let out the frustration of no one understanding, no one seeing his side, but nothing comes. How could no one recognize he was doing what his mom would have done? He's a fighter, like her. Another breath, another scream.

Another nothing. He squeezes the pillow, clenching it like it was holding him to the world. Every muscle tenses and stays tight, finally letting go when someone knocks on his door.

"Go away," he calls out through the pillow.

"It's me." Nico says through the door.

"What do you want?"

Nico comes in, "You able to breathe like that?" Eric pulls his face out of the pillow, looking away as Nico sits on the bed, "Let's talk about what happened."

"What's there to talk about? I got in a fight, I'm grounded. The end." Eric flops to his back and stares at the ceiling.

"Eric, why did you do it?"

"I don't know. Jackson was pushing Andy around and I can't stand bullies."

"Eric, you can't keep doing this. You're going to get kicked out of school."

"I don't care. What's the point? Everyone's leaving anyway."

"That's not true." Nico turns toward him. "I'm not leaving." Pausing, Nico watches Eric to see if he notices anything different in his voice. The letter from Arbor University wasn't a surprise. He had applied, after all, and he knew he'd get in. But now wasn't the time to discuss another major family change.

"You will when you go to college." Eric grumbles under his breath.

Nico relaxes hearing the theoretical nature of Eric's statement. He didn't know.

"Maybe, but that doesn't mean I'm giving up on Junction Hollow."

"What can you do? It's just you. No one else cares." Eric rolls over to see Nico's answer. "No one's going to stop the factory from shutting down. No one's going to save this town."

"I'm not giving up." Nico says, "I'm organizing a protest rally."

"For who?" Eric chuckles.

"The point is to raise awareness and maybe get people to change their minds." Nico shrugs. He goes to Eric's record player, "Why do you have mom's old records?" Nico spins the square record sleeve in his hands.

"Sounds better than that digital crap." Eric sits up, watching the record. The spinning slows, and Eric fights the urge to reach for it before it falls. Not that Nico would drop it on purpose, but those records were special to Eric. They weren't special to mom because if they were, she would have taken them. No one leaves special things behind, only things that can be forgotten.

"Sometimes the old ways are better." Nico pulls out the record and places it on the record player. He puts the sleeve back in the box. "Well, a protest in person is an old way to do it. People will come."

"Not Anna." Eric mutters under his breath. Electronic dance music thumps from the speakers.

Nico bobs his head to the beat. "Ah, the real reason-"

"No!" Eric barks. "I didn't even know she was leaving yet."

"She's leaving?" The bass trembles through the floor. A steady beat pounding like a heart quickening to a thunderous crescendo.

"Then you need to tell her how you feel."

"What's the point? No one stays in this town. No protest helps. Nothing's going to stop people from leaving."

"Is this really about Mom?" Nico turns the music down to a low pulse of warbling electronica.

Eric flops back down, rolls away, "She left."

"It wasn't our fault." Nico says, sharp and crisp. The clarity cuts through the music with a hard edge of certainty. So certain that Nico believed it. It was true, her *leaving wasn't 'our' fault.*

Eric shrugs that off. He remembers the morning she left for work and never came home. Dad said she had a business trip, but there was arguing the night before. Nico arguing with Mom, then Dad arguing with Mom. When she got ready for work the next day, Eric knew something was off and he should have said something like I love you, but he didn't. He just watched her drive away. He didn't fight.

Eric curls into a ball on his bed. "Can you shut the door on your way out?"

***

Nico nods, spins the music's volume up to let the beat thrum in Eric's mind. That's what he needs right now to get lost in the beat. He'll come back when he's ready to talk, ready to think, but until then, best to leave him alone. He knew Eric was like Mom. Sometimes they just needed to burn off steam and when they were done, they came back to talk.

How much steam did Mom needed to burn off? How much steam could be left a year later?

"He needs a bit." Nico leans on his dad's desk. "Just got a lot on his mind."

Dad nods.

"There is something—" Nico goes to the posters and reaches under the pile to the letter from Arbor University. A knock at the front door snaps his attention away from the letter.

"Can you get that? I've gotta finish this up." Dad says and turns to his keyboard.

The clacking of keyboard keys starts as Nico goes to the door, pulls it open. His jaw drops as he stares at the girl on the porch. *What is she doing here?*

4

"Hi Nico, I'm here to see Eric," Anna says. She sways on the doormat, her hands half in her pockets, her eyes glittering with the intensity that always accompanied her.

"He's, uh, not really in the mood for visitors." Nico stammers.

"I'll be quick." Anna steps forward. Nico steps back. Anna's always been intimidating. Was it her height? Her background in martial arts? No, it was her constant, unwavering focus. Everything she set her sights on, she achieved. No school record was too far from her reach. She collected achievements with the fierocity of an afficionato and, once achieved, she dismissed the accomplishments as something anyone could do.

Nico looks over his shoulder. Dad watches from his desk. He nods approval.

"Okay, for a bit." Nico says.

"I won't stay long." She smiles and pushes through, polite but determined.

"Would you like a drink?"

She shakes her head and points to the source of the throbbing electronica, "Is that still Eric's room?" She smiles. Nico nods. That's the room where her and Eric used to play dolls years ago. Nico would babysit Anna while her dad needed time to be alone. Anna handled her mother's death with the same strength that you see from her today and Nico guessed she had to be strong because her dad fell apart.

Nico pounds on the door, "It's me and a friend."

Eric doesn't answer.

Nico opens the door, waves for Anna to go in. Eric rolls over about to bark but Anna's glowing brown skin and big smile stop him.

"Hey!" Anna shouts over the music. "I just wanted to say—" Nico turns the music down with Anna still shouting. She blushes, restarts, "I wanted to say it was really cool how you stood up for Andy today." Anna looks to the record player like it's an alien technology. She cocks her head to the side and studies the spinning record. Eric springs to his feet and turns it off.

"Oh, uh, okay." Eric says.

Nico smiles and steps behind Anna. He rolls his hands, telling Eric to go on, talk to her. But Eric only stares in pathetic dreamy silence.

Nico jumps in to save Eric from his daze, "I heard you're leaving Junction Hollow?"

Anna nods, looking to the floor, "My dad got a job in Richardsport."

"When you guys moving?" Nico asks.

"The end of the month." Anna said.

"Uh, but, uh," Eric's hands flail around him, trying to grab onto the words that can't form in his head, "That's the end of the week?"

"That's Saturday." Anna shrugs.

"That's soon." Eric tries to smile, tries to make it a joke, but his voice cracks under the strain to do either.

Anna agrees, keeping her eyes away from him, "Yeah, I was surprised too."

Nico rolls his eyes and sighs in frustration. The awkward silence begs for someone to interject, for someone to say something that's not a nod or glance, "Well, Richardsport is pretty cool." He chuckles, Richardsport is where Arbor University is located. *Maybe we'll be neighbors.* "There's a really great college there. I heard they have an impressive library." Nico shuffles to the door. "I'm going to get going. You guys, uh, chat it up or whatever."

Nico slips past Anna and out of Eric's room.

***

"You know, I'll still be here Friday." Anna twists her foot into the carpet. She looks at the empty walls, the bookshelf, the box of records. Pulling a record sleeve from the box, she examines it, hiding from Eric behind its large square sleeve, "Are you going to the Frosty Formal?"

Eric was planning on asking Anna to the dance. But every time he tried, something came up that stopped him. Like the other day when he was about to ask her, and he felt he had a booger hanging out, so he didn't. Then there was lunch time yesterday when he was going to ask her, but first had to check if he had any broccoli in his teeth. Then this morning when he was going to ask her, but he had to stand up to Jackson. Seems like every time it's a perfect time, something comes up.

"I don't know." Eric says. Sweat pools in his armpits, dripping down his sides, crawling into his lower back, "I'm kind of grounded right now."

Dad pokes his head in, "You can go."

Eric's sweat turns to fountains of stink pouring from his pits. *Can Anna smell me? Am I smelly right now? Why is it so hot in here?* "Oh, okay. Are you going, Anna?" Eric's voice cracks. He tugs at his shirt collar to let some cool air in, but no amount of air relieves his quickening heartbeat, or burning face.

"I was thinking about it. If someone asks me, I'd go." Anna puts the record back. Her eyes fix on him for a moment then flick away.

"Yeah." Eric wipes his hands on his pants but the sweat's still there, a second skin of nervous tension that won't come off no matter how hard he rubs, "Uh, who's going to, I mean, do you know who's going to ask you?"

Nico groans loudly outside Eric's door.

"Oh, uh… I, I don't know." Anna says.

She turns red from her hair to her throat. That confirms what Eric already kn*ew, the room was too hot, too close.*

Nico walks in, "I'm sure someone," he stares at Eric, "will ask you to the dance. Be ready Anna, because I know you'll get asked." Nico scowls at Eric, "Can I talk to my brother, please?" As she walks out, Nico wonders where the determined Anna who almost pushed her way into the house went. It's like when Anna and Eric are together, they both just melt into quiet, confused children.

Anna waves to Eric as she walks out. He smiles and looks away quickly.

"Dude, what's your problem?" Nico hisses, "She's asking you to ask her!"

"No, I just I don't know." Eric stumbles over the words. Maybe if it was just Anna leaving, he could find the strength to say something but Anna and Andy? That's a one-two punch knocking out any hope, for anything.

"Go ask her!" Nico points to the door. "You've got this man. What's the worst thing she'll say? No? That's not going to happen. Go!"

Eric grimaces and grumbles. Nico stomps and points harder. Eric knows when his brother won't stop. Next, Nico will make signs, hold a rally, storm town hall, organize a protest if Eric doesn't go now. He gets up and trudges off to Anna, bracing for the harsh impact of rejection.

"Anna?" Eric pokes his head out the front door catching her on the welcome mat.

"Yeah?" Anna looks up from her phone, hopeful. Smiling.

The air gets thicker. It's like peanut butter pressing into Eric's lungs. The world shrinks as Anna gets bigger, and bigger, a giant filling his mind, stealing the air around him. Stealing the space. What's the worst thing she can say? But the answer is obvious. No. No is the worst thing that could happen, and it is likely to happen. It is certain to happen. She'll say no. She'll laugh. She's taking up the entire world now and all Eric can see, smell, think is NO.

"I'll let you know if I'm going to the dance." Abandoning the ask, letting breath back into his lungs.

"Oh, okay then." Anna nods, disappointed, but all Eric can see is her shrinking back to normal size. The room returning.

Anna steps off the mat, turns back, "Well, okay then. I'll see you around?"

Eric reaches out to stop her. "Wait, Anna." A moment of air let Eric find the words to say, they flew into his mind and demanded to be said before she left. She turned towards him and Eric took a deep breath.

5

Around Anna, the world fades to white as Eric is lost in her perfect, hopeful smile. Her bouncing curls. Her perfect teeth… perfect teeth.

"You have something in your teeth." The right words didn't come out, that's not what he wanted to say, but sometimes we don't control what falls through our lips.

Anna sinks, shields her teeth and nods, blushing. "Oh, thanks." She hurries down the sidewalk away from Eric's door.

WHACK!

Nico smacks the back of Eric's head.

"Are you kidding me!? You have something in your teeth? That's what you say to a gorgeous girl who wants you to ask her out?"

"What else is there to say?" Eric grumbles and rubs the back of his head. There were a lot of other things to say, and all more impactful than noting what was in her teeth. Too many thoughts collided, not enough room to think in the traffic jam of ideas. He should have said how her laughing made class bearable. How her eyes could stop traffic. How he wanted her to stay.
But he said nothing important. Did nothing to convince her to stay.
"She's leaving! End of story!" Eric screamed at Nico, his face now red from the bloody cocktail of rage and disappointment. He hur-

ries to his room, slams the door, and turns the music back on. The bass envelops him but doesn't drown his frustration.

The list of everyone who has left Junction Hollow only gets longer. Vinnie left when his dad got transferred to another factory. Mark, Lizzie, and Lonnie left when Schleppy's downsized their sheet metal shop. They were good friends who came to all Eric's birthday parties. After they left and Jackson turned into a jerk, the last ones standing were Anna, Andy, and Greenie. Soon only Greenie after Anna and Andy leave… just like his mom left.

Would Anna stay if he asked her? Would that change anything?

Nico comes in, "Dude, what's your problem? She's getting ready to leave. You've been wanting to ask her out since, like, fifth grade. This is your last chance."

Eric doesn't answer. Nico turns off the music and flops down on the bed beside Eric. "You just need to find your mojo. A little time in nature will help you forget about all the crap that's been happening."

A little time in nature' is how their mom used to say, go for a hike in the woods. Eric needs the hike, but it won't change Anna leaving. Or how Nico will leave for college. Maybe it's time to accept that everyone leaves and move on… without his mojo?

Eric sighs and climbs out of bed. Nico won't take no for an answer and instead of drawing it out, Eric accepts his fate. "Okay. Where we going?"

Nico tosses Eric his empty backpack from school. "Pack some snacks. We're going to the mountain."

Eric freezes at that. Mirror Mountain pulls him back to when things were good. When his mom and dad were still together.

When he didn't have such a lonely future. But something digs at his mind like a fingernail chipping away at paint. Large flakes fall away quickly exposing the raw, ominous feeling making his hands tremble.

"C'mon," Nico slings a backpack over his shoulder, "it'll be fun."

Fun doesn't describe the sinking feeling in Eric's gut. Something is waiting for him at Mirror Mountain. *I'm not coming back.* He shivers as the idea hits him hard, clear, and complete. Why am I thinking that? Eric shakes his head. Bad mood, bad thoughts, but the thought took root before it could be dismissed. There it sprouted and tickled Eric's mind, triggering his alarms.

"Let's go," Nico says, his excitement silencing Eric's alarms. "It's going to be an adventure."

Eric takes a deep breath and follows Nico out of the house. He knows this will be an adventure they'll never forget... but will it be one he wants to remember?

Legend says if you make a wish at the top of Mirror Mountain, your wish will come true.

"Yeah..." Eric forms the wish in his mind. "Fun."

6

Nico drives into the shadow of Mirror Mountain. Crossing into the darkness stirs the bubbling culdron of Eric's memories. Trips with Mom and Dad to the mountain float up to the surface. His mom walking off ahead of them. HIs dad saying to give her space. Entrances to the old coal mines they'd find but never go in. Dad's stories of Junction Hollow being a coal mining town decades ago. Once the coal mines were shut down, Schleppy's moved in and gave everyone jobs, making sheet metal. Now Schleppy's is offshoring and sending all the jobs over to wherever people work cheaper than here. People leave. But that's not the only reason to leave Junction Hollow… they leave because there's no reason to stay.

Nico pulls off the road and wedges his little blue car through some trees. Smooth road gives to a hard bounce and splashing mud sheets coating the trees around them.

"What are you doing?" Eric straightens up in his seat and rolls up his window.

"Searching for adventure." Nico says. He points in front of the car as they bounce along the unpaved trail, "There's a trail here. We can take it deeper into the mountain and start—"

"Somewhere other people don't start." Eric finishes the explanation their mom always gave when she did this same thing. Drive into the woods and then hike from somewhere no one else is. "We can go back to the parking area." Eric leans against his door, ignoring the waves of mud crashing over his window from the bumps and puddles in the trail.

"Nah, this is the start of the fun part." Nico smiles, "Besides, getting away is going to be good for you. Clear your head a bit." The car bounces over the rough trail but quickly the trail fades to grass and rocks as late afternoon bleeds into early evening. The mountain hides the sun, but the sky is still blue as the woods grow murky in long sunset shadows.

When the trail is completely gone for ten, maybe twenty minutes and all they can smell is the thick scent of growing things, Nico parks the car. Eric opens his and slams into a tree with a plastic pop.

"Oh, man! Sorry, Nico!" Eric slithers out the door.

"It's okay," Nico says, "We can park here." He opens his door and steps out into the woods. Eric follows, his eyes jumping from car to the mountain towering over them. His neck pops as it stretches to see through the trees up the mountain.

"This is stupid." Eric pulls on his backpack, "Night's coming soon." A bruise purple sky creeps into the world around them.

"We've been up here tons at night," Nico says, "And we've been alone a few times, too." He hands Eric a flashlight and a bottle of water. "Come on, let's go."

Eric makes sure his phone is on him before he steps away from the car. He glances at his signal strength. Two bars. He remembers seeing a news article about the cell phone towers on Mirror Mountain and how they kept breaking. Something about signal relay

strength or electromagnetic phenomenon. That's why calls in Junction Hollow always sound like crap. Better signal strength, another reason to leave.

***

The hike up Mirror Mountain isn't for what Nico calls, "Rail Trail Runners." People who love flat trails, would have a heart attack hiking this steep incline full of down trees and rocks jutting out to slice your shoes. Nothing about this hike is easy. The terrain is rough, the choking humidity of a coming storm makes them strain to breath. And worst of all, the nerve rattling bugs buzz and scream their discordant songs preparing for rain.

As Nico and Eric climb higher, Eric's thoughts drift further away from Junction Hollow, making room for peace to settle over him. The day's events are crunched and crushed out of Eric's mind with each step through the forest deadfall. Even the thoughts of Andy and Anna leaving evaporate with the heavy scent of evening dew gathering over the grass. New thoughts tumble back to Eric. Thoughts of Nico and happy memories of Mom and Dad walking up the mountain.

Eric laughs, "Hey Nico," he says through a heavy breath, "remember when Dad ate that nasty tuna sandwich?"

Nico laughs and clicks on his flashlight, "Yeah, and he tried to get us to eat it, too."

"I thought Mom was going to kill him when she realized what happened." Eric climbs over a large rock, "She was so mad. Especially when he puked on the trail."

"Yeah, I know. You'd think he'd of stopped eating the tuna when he saw the furry mold. Remember him pointing it out to us?" Nico slows his pace, shines the flashlight in front of him, then back behind him. "Uh, whoa." Nico stops laughing and dodges something in the tree. Eric bumps into him, bounces off and sees the shadow of what Nico ran into.

Both their flashlights jump to the tree branches clawing down towards them. Dangling from the tree are twisted sticks tied together to make faceless people. Countless figures hang from the tree by strings tied to their arms like lifeless puppets waiting to come alive. But the tree doesn't need to move, the frozen gusts of wind blowing down the mountain make the figures dance. They dance with the ecstatic joy of being found, of being seen.

Eric's stomach drops as one of the stick figures reaches for him. He jumps away, shining his light on it, The figure is just blowing in the wind. Not coming to life. Not trying to grab him.

Each figure is paired with another. Their strings wrap into each other in a tight coil that splits to appear like the Scales of Justice. Eric tugs on one figure. "Whoa." Letting go, the figure bounces up and dances around, the paired figure sways and bounces in sync. "Weird." Eric runs his hand through the bunches of figures, sending them all into motion.

"Pretty cool." Nico nods, "Probably someone's art project from the Community College or something." Nico presses his face to one set of the figures, "Check out the coloring. The wood is the same color for the figures on this branch." Nico tucks the flashlight in his armpit and grabs the two figures in both hands. "Look, they are like exactly the same. Even the sticks that make them up are broken in the same places."

Eric comes over. Sees it. Looks up to the night sky. Stars break through tree canopy. "Want to head back?"

"Freaked out?" Nico chuckles and makes ghost noises.

"No, just didn't want to be out all night." Eric rolls his eyes and pushes his brother but he can't stop looking at the twin stick figures. They're watching him. Swaying back away from him, inviting him to walk through them. And not just these two in front of Nico but all of them dancing in the wind. Many are low enough to be seen but many more are in the higher branches, too high to reach without climbing the tree but Eric didn't see any branches low enough to start a climb. How did they get up there? He stared at the dancing figures, stepping back aways from their invitation to enter.

"You got other plans?" Nico asks, "Oh, wait, no, because you're grounded and suspended." Nico laughs and pushes through the wall of dancing stick figures.

Eric sighs, swallows hard, and follows. One figure holds on as he passes through, tugging at Eric's jacket. "What?" Turning back, Eric pulls the figure loose, releases it. The stick figure dances and clatters against its twin in a hollow clacking.

Is it laughing? Eric wonders as he listens to the sound of the figures colliding in their wild dance. The clacking, the cackling, of the stick people behind him makes his skin ripple in goosebumps. It's not the wind. Not the gust of icy air but those figures…celebrating.

"Eric?" Nico whispers.

Eric jumps and turns. All joy evacuated from Nico's as he nods toward an old mining shack. Moonlight paints the shack in pale blue with deep black shadows accenting every angle. Orange lights glow inside the shack. The mists stretch the light out from the shack in soft halos.

"Where'd that come from?" Eric whispers and points to the shack, "Like, shouldn't we have seen that a while ago? Not like there's anything else around here."

Nico shrugs, clears his throat to ensure Eric doesn't get too freaked out. "Probably a camper. Just turned on their lantern or something." Nico keeps walking. They approach the dilapidated shack slowly. "Want to say hi?" Nico smiles and flips the flashlight up under his chin, giving him a ghostly face and hoping the joke will break Eric's darkening mood.

But before Eric can answer, the shack's door creaks open.

7

A small person wearing dirty overalls with long stringy black hair around his face waddles out of the shack. He turns toward them, holds up a lantern, letting the orange glow show his boyish face and torn up clothes.

Eric thinks it looks like a high school kid. *Isn't it too late for a school night?* Nico shouldn't be up here this late. Why's this kid hanging out alone in a creepy shack?

"Hello?" Eric calls out.

A long sigh comes from the kid. His shoulders shrink in defeat. Eric hears something running in the dark outside the lantern glare. The stick figure that held onto his jacket comes to mind. It laughed as he pulled free. It danced with all its friends. Eric shivered. *Did the stick figures come to life? Are they chasing us?*

Nico spins to spot whatever made the noise, but only glimpses a shadow running. "Probably a deer?" Nico says. The uncertainty in his voice sends another shiver quaking through Eric. Nico has never been a good liar. *Did Nico know what it was?*

"Don't be scared." Eric says, trying to project confidence but failing. In the orange halos coming from the shack, Eric sees Nico scanning the trees with his flashlight. He hears the shadows too.

The kid turns back to them. His dark eyes drift to the ground, avoiding them. "I'm Tommy."

"Nice to meet you, Tommy," Nico says.

Eric studies Tommy's face and notices his mouth is stuck in a frown, as if he's in pain.

"We're just out exploring," Eric explains.

Tommy's eyes slowly drift up to meet Eric's, "You shouldn't be here," his voice is a harsh whisper, like he doesn't want to be overheard, "it's not safe."

Nico pulls the flashlight close to himself, keeping it on Tommy, but it doesn't stop his hand from trembling. "What do you mean?"

Eric remembers the car parked down the road. He checks his phone. No cell signal. No bars. And now, no GPS.

"You guys shouldn't be here," Tommy repeats and shuffles back into the shack. "Mirror Mountain lies." His voice fades as he disappears inside. "Go! If you still can," he whispers.

A branch snaps beside Eric. He spins with his flashlight. The light catches two glowing eyes, animal eyes, and then the animal runs off.

Eric whispers, "Did you see that?"

But Nico's mind is on Tommy's last words. "What did he mean by that?" his voice trembling. "Did he say, 'if we can?'"

"I don't know." Eric shines the flashlight around. He doesn't see anything but hears the dead fall crunching under something's feet. He feels the unblinking stare of something watching him. *The stick people.* He tries to shake away the thought, but it doesn't leave. Mist blankets the forest floor in a dark haze, hiding the world below Eric's shins. "We should probably go."

Nico nods, his face pale in the moonlight. "Yeah, let's go."

Eric and Nico start back the way they came. After a few minutes, they realize they're lost. Noises follow them, stalk them through the woods just outside their flashlight's reach.

Nico holds his phone up higher, trying to get a GPS signal. "What's going on here?" His phone blurts at him as he refreshes for a signal. Nico restarts his phone. Eric does the same.

No signal found. No GPS, no cellular, no wi-fi. Nothing. Only the faint rustling noises surrounding them.

"Where's the car?" Eric points his flashlight to the ground and looks for their tracks. Footprints in the mud? Snapped branches? Anything to show him how to get back home. Every tree looked new. The path is fresh, as if no one has walked it before.

Panic sets into Eric's heart, making it thump harder, louder. They need to get out of these woods before the stick people catch them. Reason steps in, assuring Eric there are no stick people and those were just sculptures, like Nico said. Someone's art project and not monsters in the dark. But reason can't stand in the face of darkness and fear *when you're* lost in the woods.

"We have to keep moving," Nico says.

Eric follows Nico, their flashlight beams bouncing as they run. The noises around them get louder, closing in.

"There's no way we are going to make it back to the car," Eric says. "But if we keep moving, maybe we can outrun whatever is following us." The crunching branches get louder and both snap around to see what's breathing down their neck.

But all that is behind them is Tommy's shack.

"We've been going for at least," Eric looks at his phone, "thirty minutes. How are we still here?" Eric looks at the shack. They are right in front of the door. Right where they were talking to Tommy.

"I don't know." Nico scans the dark with his flashlight.

Eric looks back the way they came. "We have to keep moving."

Nico nods and they take off into the woods again, running as fast as they can toward their car. But no matter how fast or hard they run, it doesn't get them any closer to the car. Every time they turn around, the shack is there.

Panting, Nico bangs on the door. "Hey! You in there!"

Tommy answers. His face is bored, shoulders slumped. "Yes?"

"What did you mean when you said escape while we could?" Nico demands.

Tommy sighs. "I told you, don't come here." Tommy closes the shack's door. Nico slams his hand on the door, pushing it back open. Tommy startles at the contact.

Eric smiles and backs off his brother. Normally, Eric's the aggressor and Nico's the pacificist. Not this time.

"What's going on here!?" Nico barks.

Eric watches the forest, listening to the noise of something. No, not something, some things, two things running in the woods away from them. Running up the mountain.

"Mirror Mountain is haunted. You can't leave until you go to the top of the mountain." Tommy's face finally breaks from bored. His mouth dips into a regret-filled frown. "There are spirits racing you

to the top of the mountain. If they get there and then back here before you, they will take over your life and you'll be stuck here with me."

Nico's face twists in disbelief. "What? That's total —"

Eric tugs at Nico's arm, "We need to go, Nico." Branches crackle up the mountain. Eric swings his flashlight toward the sound, but it fades as whatever is running gets further away. "I believe in ghosts enough to not want to find out. Let's go!"

Back in Eric's room, he felt this. Dread was building in him, and now it was here. Eric had never been ghost hunting or worried about the supernatural, but there was no doubt in his mind now. The stick figures had come to life and whatever Tommy was talking about, Eric didn't want to just let whatever happens next happen without a fight.
"Good luck. If you meet Mastermind, please ask him if I can leave yet." Tommy closes his door with a quiet sigh. Nico runs up the mountain towards the sounds. Eric follows.

Laughing breaks the constant snapping and crunching of the woods. It rolls down the mountain like an avalanch of sinister glee but it's familiarity makes Nico and Eric freeze. It is Eric's laugh, but Eric isn't laughing.

8

"Eric?" Nico staggers back. "Did you…?"

Eric shook his head. "Not me." Eric looks at his brother and then at the surrounding woods. Their flashlights jump around to see who's laughing, but no one's there. They only hear the crunching and cracking of someone running further and faster away. "We can't lose whoever that is."

"We'll get them! Whatever's going on, we've got this." The old Nico returns with a burst of positivity. Nico's positivity is always a beacon for Eric. It's why he always looks up to his brother, the guy who can see the best in everything and everyone, even when they don't see the best in you.

They run to catch up to whoever is ahead of them. Their flashlights catch shoes, but Eric thinks that was just his imagination. *It's just some kids playing pranks.* Eric keeps thinking about that, but his gut tells him something different. What they're chasing isn't human. It's not an animal. It's not natural.

"WHOA!" Nico grabs Eric, ripping him backward away from the cliff. Thoughts of ghosts and curses kept him from noticing the drop, kept him from hearing the rushing water between this cliff and the next. A stream cut through the mountain with a fallen tree bridge resting for anyone to cross.

"We need to cross." Eric looks at the river, then at his brother.

The fall isn't far. Not a death on impact fall. More like a 'get swept away and drown in the current' fall.

"I'll go first." Nico pushes some rocks off the tree with his foot. They plop into the water with a splash. Nico steps on it carefully, testing if it will hold his weight.

"Nico!" Eric's voice hits the high notes, only found in deep panic. "That tree is rotten!"

"We've got this, Eric." Nico keeps walking, toe to heel. His arms reach out to the sides, grabbing the air for balance as he slowly crosses, swaying side to side. His foot slips. He regains balance quickly. "Careful," Nico gasps, "slippery here." He points to the spot on the log.

Eric takes note.

Nico crosses the log and breathes out as his foot hits the other side. He looks back at Eric. "Your turn. You can do this, Eric."

Eric nods and follows his brother. Each step speeds up his heartbeat until his fingers tingle and neck throbs with each pulse. The water is louder than before. Icy droplets jump up and bite at his hands, signalling the pain that awaits if he slips. A constant rush of water crashing against the rocks makes it hard to think.
He passes the slick spot, taking a breath as he steps over it with a heavy footfall on the other side. That's when he feels a crack where his foot hit the tree. Panic floods Eric's mind as the tree groans, threatening to break. He looks down and sees that it is rotten with age and wear, splinters of wood breaking off in places where his weight presses down, "I'm not going to make it."

"Yes you are!" Nico barks, waving Eric towards him, "You've got this!"

Rot cascades down from the log. Nico's flashlight focuses on it. Eric's thoughts can't get out of the noise of the stream, the cracking of the log. All he can think is MOVE. He steps, the trunk shifts down, splintering under him. Eric slips. He catches the log, his feet hitting the water.

"Eric!" Nico shouts and reaches for him.

Eric stretches his arm to reach him as the rotten log gives way, cracking with thunderous finality as Eric plunges into the stream. The pain is instant and engulfing as icy water submerges him, squeezes all the breath out of him and leaves the needles of hypothermia deep in his bones. His head pops out of the water. Nico is above him on the ridge, running after him. The water overtakes Eric again.

Eric tries to yell but his lungs fill with water. The mountain goes dark as he's drug under the current. His body slamming into rocks on the stream bed. They spin him around, slash his elbow, dunking him like an uncaring bully at a pool party. He can't scream through the water in his mouth. Can't see through the darkness suffocating him.

He flails in the water, trying to find the surface, anything to keep him alive, but there's only darkness and the unyielding water. A hard smash into a sharp rock knocks the fight out of Eric. His body goes limp from the impact. Thoughts explode in his mind, confirming his fate. He's going to die here. In this stream. Die alone, abandoned by everyone. His eyes close as he slips into unconsciousness, letting the water take him away.

"Hey!" a voice says as hands shake him awake, "You okay?"

Mud smears across Eric's face, clumping in his eye lashes as he turns over on the river bed shore. He pushes against the craggy rocks to get up but can't get the strength in his numb legs. He's on the shore. *I must have washed up downstream?*

Eric blinks through the mud in his eyelashes. A blurry figure is standing over him. "Nico?"

9

"Yeah," Nico sighs, "thought you were a goner." He stands over Eric. Moonlight glitters in Nico's blonde hair, but that's all Eric can see through mud covered eyes.

Eric sighs relief, Nico's here. He didn't leave. He didn't let Eric go. "Where's the flashlight?"

"Gone, I guess," Nico shrugs, "washed away when you fell."

"Can't see anything," Eric says. "What happened?" He palms wads of mud away from his face, throwing them into the river.

"You hit your head pretty hard on a rock." Nico replies, "Lucky for you, I found you before you drowned. But by now, those others are almost at the top of the mountain. They've probably won."

"Won what?" Eric reaches for his phone. He tugs it out of his soaking wet pocket and taps the flashlight looking up the mountain. The sinking feeling crashes back into his guts, remembering what Tommy said pops in his mind getting him out of the mud and to his feet, "I wasn't out long. Let's go. We can make it!" Eric runs up the hill.

"Fine." Nico trudges along behind him.

Eric and Nico race up the moonlit mountain. Eric determined to catch whoever is laughing at them further up the trail, Nico plodding along. Tommy said they were chasing spirits. Apparently,

45

the ghosts are thinking funny thoughts or laughing at Eric's fall. Whatever's so funny, the laughing doesn't stop. It's taunting, malicious, pleading to be caught.

Eric hears someone running behind them. Whoever is back there fades away, staying at the river moving down stream, while the person upstream runs faster.

"You can't catch me!" The voice taunts. Eric runs harder, his lungs burning as he tries to catch up. But whoever's up there is too fast. Their laughter ringing in Eric's ears. "You'll never catch me!"

"What's going on?" Nico says breathlessly. "We're never going to catch that guy."

Eric speeds up. "That's not a good attitude." Eric remembers Nico telling him the same thing earlier, "We've almost caught them." Eric wondered, *who is up there? Some kids pranking me and Nico? Real ghosts?* Eric thought it might be the second. Something felt wrong. This mountain felt wrong.

The person ahead of them is just a blob of shadow, but Erics sees them dive into a dark hole in the mountain. Eric follows without hesitation. He slides down a long, dark tunnel on his stomach, his hands gripping the smooth stone edges to slow himself down. A pink glowing is at the end of the tunnel. Eric slides down slowly and comes out into a large cavern.

Nico shouts down from above him, "What are you doing?"

Eric's eyes are drawn to the giant pink gem floating in the center of the open cavern. It glows, throwing pale light around the room. "I think I found," Eric considers the giant gemstone, "treasure, maybe?" Eric looks to the walls, seeing carvings in a strange language he can't recognize. "It's safe. Come on down." The carvings aren't just language but pictograms telling a story like the cave paintings he saw in history class. But these carvings aren't messy, they are precise in sharp angles, either carved by a master craftsman or a machine.

"I don't know." Nico whines.

"Just get down here." Eric barks and shines his phone up the tunnel. He sees Nico's feet climbing down.

"Oh, man," Nico breathes as he comes to stand next to Eric, "what is this place?"

Eric shines his light around the cavern, taking in the carvings, the gem, and two doors. One a wooden door has a symbol carved into the top that looks like stalactites and an hourglass. Another door is across the room, the gem between the two doors. This second door is made of metal with a brass handle.

Eric looks at the symbol on the metal door and then at the gem, "I," he runs his fingers over the carving on the brass handle, "I know what this means," he says softly.

"What?" Nico asks.

"This is a trial," Eric says, looking at the carving: Two scales, one with a heart and one with a feather, "The Trial of Ma'at. We learned about this in history. Egyptian mythology."

"You are correct, Eric of Junction Hollow." The gem pulses as a voice booms through the cavern. Pebbles fall from the ceiling, bouncing off Eric's head.

"Who said that?" Eric whirls around with his phone, looking for who else is in the cavern. The ghost?

"I said that." The gem pulses again. Eric stares at it as Nico comes up beside him. "I am Mastermind, Keeper of Mirror Mountain, and the terrors or treasures below."

"What the—" Eric turns to Nico, but his words die as he sees Nico doesn't have a face. Blonde hair falls around a featureless bulge like a pale mannequin face. "Ahhh!" Eric drops his phone. It cracks on the rock floor and echoes through the room.

"What?" No Face Nico says.

Mastermind laughs, "Not who you were expecting, Eric?"

IO

"Where's Nico!" Eric screams. He rushes to the door with the brass handle, shaking the handle frantically to open it. But it's locked, the gem glowing brightly in front of him.

"Ah ah ah," Mastermind taunts, "You cannot leave until you know the rules of the trial."

Eric lets go of the handle. Stepping back, he sees the scale again with the heart and feather. He turns towards Nico, who is still standing there with a blank expression on his nothing face. "What did you do to Nico?"

"That's not your brother," Mastermind says. "When you crossed the Wall of Twins, the Trial of Mirror Mountain began. Your Mirror, some call it your Evil Twin, manifested as a mountain spirit. It came here for a body." Mastermind laughs, "Your body."

Eric shakes his head. *This isn't real. It can't be real? I'm still knocked out on the river shore…* "Wall of Twins—wait, I don't have an Evil Twin."

"Everyone has an Evil Twin, Eric." Mastermind says, "And yours is very powerful."

Eric looks at Nico and, again, at the gem. "Wall of Twins?" He shakes his head, sees the gem, shakes again, harder this time to get out of whatever hallucination he's having.

"Yes, the Wall of Twins has many manifestations throughout the forests of Mirror Mountain. It could have been a line of statues, the cave entrance carved with figures—"

"A bunch of stick figures hanging from the trees?"

"Yes. You came in the southwest entrance then." Mastermind flickers as if giggling.

"This can't be happening." But the knot in his gut tightens. The cave walls seem so real with their carvings and cool, smooth texture. Mastermind's pink glow fades, *making the carvings vanish in shadow.* "Okay, fine, assuming this isn't some kind of weird joke. I need to finish the trial?" Eric turns back to the floating gemstone. He checks for wires or speakers or something to make this trick work, but there's nothing. "Give me the rules."

Mastermind lets out a loud laugh. "At this point in the game, the rules are simple: get to the Wall of Twins before your Mirror."

"Those stick things by the shack? And if I don't?" Eric looks at No Face Nico.

"You probably won't." No Face Nico shakes his head.

Eric stared at the faceless thing. *How does it talk without a mouth?*

Mastermind chuckles, "Yes, the 'stick things' and if you don't reach the Wall of Twins before your Mirror, the Mirror becomes you. Then you are trapped on Mirror Mountain. If you get there first, the treasure of Mirror Mountain will be unlocked, and the keys released." Mastermind says. The gem pulses with each syllable. Eric waits for Mastermind to laugh. It sounds like he wants to, like something hilarious has been said. At least, Eric assumes it is a *he.* Sounds like a he.

That's what happened to Tommy. Tommy is trapped here. "If I lose, I'm trapped?"

Mastermind laughs, "Don't waste time. Ticktock Eric of Junction Hollow." The metal door with the scales slides open, revealing night sky and trees. An icy breeze weaves into the cavern, sending chills over Eric. "Oh, and beware, there are other mountain spirits that are…" Mastermind cackles a laugh, "… less friendly than a Mirror. Mirrors only want to replace you. Others want to eat you."

Eric squints to keep out the gushing, frozen air as he runs into the night. His jaw tightens and ears perk up at the sounds of the forest all around him. The woods are no longer silent. No longer just people running. Now, there are other things. Branches snap above him. Dirt billows in the moonlight far from his trail. Eric feels the eyes that have awoken to him. He hears their panting hunger. He feels the ground rumble as they stand and stalk towards him.

But No Face Nico doesn't follow right away. He turns to Mastermind, "You didn't tell him about the other trials?"

Mastermind slowly dims, letting the cavern drift into shadow. "One trial at a time. Those are the rules. For now."

No Face Nico strolls after Eric, leaving the cave's darkness as Mastermind goes silent.

II

"This is totally crazy!" Eric screams into the night. Gravity speeds up his sprint as he descends the mountain. A flood of noises surrounds him. Countless things in the woods chasing him, but their chase helps keep his legs motivated to move faster. Master-mind said the things chasing him were mountain spirits. Eric didn't want to find out what they looked like, what they were, or how close they were. He just wanted to escape.

He's done with crazy. He just wants to find Nico. Go home and never go hiking again. Eric knew driving to nowhere was a bad idea. Mom had bad ideas like this all the time. She called them adventures, but he never felt adventurous. He felt like they were hiking to nowhere. Running to nothing, just to figure out they were lost.

And now he's here. Running through the woods. Chased by mountain spirits. Trying to stop his evil twin from taking over his life and ruining the last few days he had with Anna. Eric snorted a laugh, thinking how crazy that sounded. He might be actually lost on the mountain but for the first time this year, he doesn't feel lost. Now he has a purpose. He has direction: Get back to the Wall of Twins, the creepy stick figure things. For once, he knew what to do and why. That was refreshing.

So much about the last year was 'why'? Why did mom leave? Why didn't I say anything? Why, why, why? But now the why of what to do was answered. Why beat his evil twin down the mountain? It still sounded absurd, but he knew the answer, to take control of his life. If the evil twin was real, Eric didn't want to give up what little he had left for the few days he had left.

But the good energy that came with his feeling of purpose was quickly stomped out by a more familiar feeling, being alone. Someone had always been there for him, but not now. As he ran down Mirror Mountain, he ran alone hoping to find the real Nico, but knowing that this trial is for him and him alone. He didn't know how he knew that, but he did just like he knew not to come here. Nico didn't have to beat his mirror, Eric did. And Eric's mirror had a head start.

"Eric!?" It was Nico's scream, but was it Nico?

"Go away!" Eric screamed back. He didn't slow, but sped up. No time to waste with No Face Nico.

"What? Hey! Wait!" An iron grip seized Eric's arm, stopping his run down the mountain, "I thought you drowned!" Nico ripped Eric into a squeezing hug, "Don't you ever do that again!"

Eric ripped away from the hug. "Get off me!" Eric looked back. The mountain spirits were right behind him, but now, they're silent. Glowing eyes, dim and dusty haze evaporated as a cloud covered the moon.

"What is wrong with you!?" Nico shouted, "What's going on!?"

"Look into the moonlight." Eric pointed up as the moon came back out.

"Why?"

"Just do it." Eric growled.

Nico looks up. The moonlight caught his nose, sparkled over his tear-streaked cheeks and glittered in his eyes.

"You're really Nico?" Eric grabbed his brother's arms.

"Of course I am." Nico shook his head. "Who else would I be?"

A screech split the reunion as both Eric and Nico glance up the mountain. The mountain spirits' pursuit was restarting in a horde of shapeless shadows in the trees, tumbling mounds of mud and dirt, barreling towards them.

"I'll tell you while we run!" Eric tugs his brother's arm forward down the mountain. Nico doesn't hesitate and goes with him.

"What's going on?" Nico asks as they run.

"I found my Mirror, and he's been trying to take over my life." Eric explains, "But I won't let him. I'm going to beat him in a trial set by Mastermind."

"A trial!?" Nico yelps. "I didn't understand any of that." Nico shakes his head.

"Yeah, I don't get it either. For now, we've got to get back to the stick figure thing we saw earlier tonight. That's down the mountain, so we go down the mountain."

They get to the river. The broken remains of the log bridge, the parts that haven't washed away in the river, sit below them.

"Oh, man." Eric pants for breath. "Now what?"

"We gotta find another way down." Nico looks around them. "Another bridge?"

Eric sees the mountain spirits coming towards them again. He can feel their shadowy eyes on him, stalking him. "Nico, we've got company."

Nico's breath catches in his throat as he follows Eric's gaze. His eyes widen in horror. The dark forms that emerge are a twisted amalgamation of mountain creatures. They would have been beautiful in their own right, but now melded together into monstrous aberrations.

A slender, russet fur-covered body is supported by eight grotesque, spindly legs, each tipped with curved claws. Its ears are unmistakably those of a fox, twitching at every sound, while an elongated snout reveals rows of sharp fangs. Its bushy tail trails behind it, flicking with a sinister grace as it moves.

More hideous collisions of mountain animals take shape around them. Wolves with the wings and beaks of eagles, deer with the scales and venomous fangs of snakes, rabbits with the horns and hooves of mountain goats—all of them converging on Nico and Eric with menacing intent.

"Run!" Nico pulls Eric. They sprint down stream following the river, "There's got to be another way. Your Mirror is going somewhere."

Eric sees someone ahead of them. The boy disappears into the shadows, but Eric knows they aren't far behind his Mirror.

Neither of them dare to look back. Their eyes stay forward. Eric slips in the mud where he crawled out of the stream, but Nico catches him, and they don't miss a step. Further down the mountain, the forest fades from tall trees and dense canopy to jagged stumps and cloudy sky.

"Eric!" Nico points ahead of them as a cloud peels away from the moonlight showing a cluster of buildings. A mining town. A ghost town.

Eric sees his Mirror-his evil twin, it looks exactly like him. It has a face. Eric's face. The Mirror stands in the town square laughing at Eric running down the mountain.

"Run, run as fast as you can!" Mirror Eric screams as he takes off running again.

Eric and Nico run hard, panting with frozen lungs, into the town square. They follow MIrror Eric, assuming the Mirror knows how to get down the mountain.

"Can't catch me!" Mirror Eric's voice echoes through the empty town. The tall buildings carry it around, bouncing it along the rooftops and out the second-story windows.

This town could have been torn from a western, with the boarded-up windows and tumbleweed drifting through the street. Eric looks down main street waiting for a man in black to step out, push back his dusty trench coat and draw down on them. Rusted out mining carts were toppled throughout the town. Wooden structures, their paint now chipped and faded, lined the dusty main street. Their boarded-up windows casting solemn shadows upon the ground. Nature was reclaiming this town with shrubs pushing up through the streets. This was a ghost town, not just from being abandoned, but Eric was certain actual ghosts lurked in these buildings. That thought slowed his run, weakening his resolve to be here any longer.
Nico didn't slow. He wasn't thinking, only hunting their prey. He grabs Eric's arm and pulls him to follow the voice.
A black-winged creature blots out the moonlight, swooping down on them from a side street. It screeches, silencing the rest of the world at the moment it attacks. Eric dives over Nico, shielding his brother as they hit the ground. The talons tear into Eric's back, but he feels nothing. It screeches in anger as it swoops up and flies away.

"Are you okay?" Nico asks.

Eric nods, "Yeah, I'm fine." But Nico sees he's not fine. Blood trickles from his shoulder where the talons got him.

The ground shakes. Mirror Eric giggles, a loud, echoing giggle as the ground shakes again. An old shingle falls from a window over the SALOON sign. The moonlight casts a long shadow over Main street as a giant gray furry claw, the size of Nico's car, appears from behind a building. It slams down on Main street, sending shockwaves through Eric and Nico's knees.

Another claw slams down, shaking the ground again. Eric almost loses his balance at the quaking. Those massive claws pull a more massive body out from behind the buildings at the edge of town. It's a wolf. A gray wolf the size of a small passenger jet, armored with a black turtle's shell covering its body and head. Slowly it turns down Main street facing Eric and Nico.

It snarls, letting strands of saliva dangle down to the dirt.

Mirror Eric laughs again as the creature roars and charges at the brothers.

12

Eric and Nico bolt through the desolate mining village, their hearts racing as they flee from the towering wolf spirit. Its rancid breath surrounds them, relentless in its pursuit. Each stride they take jolts the earth beneath their feet, threatening to knock them off their course. Will they make it out alive?

The wolf spirit swipes at them, knocking them both through the Saloon's batwing doors. Loud smacking sounds clatter around them as the doors flips back and forth from their harsh entrance. The boys hit the ground hard, rolling across the floor, stopping against the saloon's back bar. Eric's head throbs, his vision blurs as he sits up. He winces, grabbing his arm.

Nico groans next to him, stirring. The wolf's claw had caught him across the back, leaving gashes in his shirt but no blood. Eric stands, but his legs feel like jelly. The wolf comes for them, its heavy footsteps galloping down the street. He had to do something. Behind them was a bar, old stools, nothing that could be a weapon. Eric jumped over the bar and looked for a gun. Western movies always had a gun behind the bar. But he didn't see any in this saloon.

The wall smashes in as the wolf spirit's snapping mouth reaches for Eric. Snarling and roaring, the wolf pushes through the wall as the wooden frame splinters and screams. Drool splashes out in foamy whips through the Saloon's interior.

"Eric!" Nico staggers to his feet, pulls Eric across the room, and throws him out the window. Walls splinter and scream from the pressure of the wolf as Nico tumbles out the window after Eric. The wolf pushes through the building, collapsing it around the creature. A claw explodes from the falling debris, swiping again as Nico pushes Eric further into the street. "Go!"

But Eric can't get his legs to work. He can't stop staring at the giant wolf spirit as it frees itself from the collapsed saloon and comes for them again. Just as the wolf burst out of the building, Eric's legs remember to run away. They find their strength, and he bolts down an alley with Nico close behind him.

The brothers run, turn a corner, turn another, then quickly, quietly sneak through a door labeled Took's General. Dust swirls as they move deeper into the darkness, it clings to their clothes, gets in their mouths. Eric brushes at his nose to keep from sneezing. *I'm not going to sneeze!* He shouts in his mind.

Nico shuts the door behind them.

Slashes of moonlight creep into the store through boarded-up windows. Eric's eyes slowly adjust to the dimness. Furniture and shelves emerge from the dark. *This was an old general store*, Eric thinks. Supplies still sat in dust coated bins lining the walls and shelves. He turns to Nico and shivers when he sees the raw fear in his brother's eyes. Nico is the guy who can conquer anything. Eric's brother. Master of positivity and the look of hopelessness on his face is what makes Eric doubt they'll make it home tonight. If Nico doubts it, then how could it be possible?

"Nico," Eric whispers, "what do we do?"

Nico shakes his head and looks around the store. Eric knows what he's looking for. A weapon. A gun. A sword. Anything. But the only thing left in this store was rotted boxes, rusted canisters, and dust. Choking clouds of dust.

That dust quakes from the shelves in gray sheets, drifting down with each thunderous step coming towards them. The wolf is getting closer. Another step sends another wave of dust to the floor. Each quake sends more waves to the floor. The steps get closer. The quakes harder.

Then they stop.

Silence holds Eric and Nico's breath captive. They don't move. Just wait. The wolf was close. They could smell its breath, but why wasn't it moving? Was it waiting for them? Seeing what they'd do?

BOOM! The room shakes as the wolf pounds on the door. The frame splinters, and the door buckles under the weight of the creature, but it holds. For now. Eric and Nico look at each other, then back at the door as it shudders under the assault.

The wolf was trying to knock the building down on them. They need another escape.

Nico runs toward the door and grabs a chair, wedging it under the handle. "It won't hold for long," he said, his voice shaking.

"We have to find a way out." Eric said.

He looks around the room, but there is no way out. The windows were boarded shut. There weren't any other doors. They were trapped in this storeroom with a giant wolf about to break through their only barrier.

They stood back as the door buckled and broke. Snarls and slobber drip through the broken door. One green eye glares through the shattered door frame, unblinking, staring, saying without words: *I've got you now.* A low growl rumbles through the floor as the wolf retracts, preparing for the final strike to break through the store and bring it all down.

"Get down! Over there!" Nico points to an area of the floor behind the store shelves. "Stay there!"

Nico grabs a stool from the counter and throws it at one of the boarded-up windows. The stool shatters on impact, but Nico doesn't stop. He rushes to the window, throwing his whole body into the boards and explodes out into the street. Eric sees him disappear out the window, climb to his feet, and start running.

"Hey! Over here you—" Nico didn't finish. The wolf spirit chases.

"No," Eric whispers, "don't leave me." He runs to the window just as the wolf passes. Eric sees the wolf spirit gaining on Nico, its giant black shell bounding up and down as it ran.

Shocked, Eric jumps out the window after them. The wolf turns to see him and growls but kept chasing Nico. Green eyes fixed on the older brother, the larger meal. Running, but not sprinting, the wolf follows Nico as he runs out of the mining town. As they leave the mining town, once called Little Hollow, the roaring river gets louder. Nico stops at a cliff jutting out over the river.

"Come on!" Nico waves for the wolf spirit to come at him.

Nico's plan becomes clear to Eric, and Eric stumbles at the thought. He falls to the ground. Nico's screaming for the wolf to come get him.

"Nico!" Eric screams.

But Nico isn't listening. Maybe he can't hear over the thunderous river or the wolf claw's quaking, but Eric didn't think either was true. He knew Nico didn't want to hear, didn't want to see him.

Eric stops, staring at his brother, wondering if this is the last time he'll see him. Eric stares at Nico, imprinting how he looks on the cliff's edge: fierce, defiant, brave, and then buries his face into the grass so he doesn't see what's next.

The wolf spirit leaps at Nico, pouncing onto him as Nico dives forward, under the wolf. It soars over the edge of the cliff, hitting the river with a tidal splash exploding up into the night sky, drenching Nico as it fell over the cliff. Nico winks at Eric like there was never any doubt.

"I'm good!" Nico shouts to get his brother's head out of the grass.

Eric sees Nico. Relief blows over him.

Nico raises his hands in victory, then vanishes as he's ripped into the stream by a giant claw. The wolf spirit was defeated, but it wasn't going alone. When it hit the water, it could still reach Nico. The brothers celebrated too soon.

Eric's joy is ripped from him as he sprints to the cliff edge. Nico sways over the edge, one hand holding onto a fallen tree as the water pelts him and pries his grip loose.

"No!" Eric screams and leans into his run, "No!" Eric is thankful his legs were still numb from before because he's never run this fast. His muscles would be burning if he could feel them, but right now he couldn't feel anything. Nothing could fit inside his mind but the fear of losing his brother. "Don't let go!" But Eric knows Nico will. Eric's seen this in the movies. This is how the sidekick dies.

Nico holds tight. Shouting through the pain of icy water smashing into him. Dragging him away. He's still holding on when Eric gets there and reaches out to him. Nico's just beyond Eric's grasp. Eric strains. The cold water is numbing Nico's hands. He tries to reach up, misses the branch. The stretch loosens his grip, fingers unable to feel the branch anymore. Nico's hand opens and the water rips him into the dark, but Eric's fingers wrap into Nico's sleeve as Eric hangs from the tree, screaming and pulling his brother out of the water.

Eric's eyes tear up as he strains, "You're not leaving me!"

Nico finds the feeling in his fingers again and grabs the tree. Eric's strength becomes his strength as Nico climbs up the tree and both Eric and Nico roll onto the cliff's edge soaking wet, freezing water clinging to their bodies, but alive.

"I'm going to win!" Mirror Eric gleefully screams up to them. He's further down the mountain and moving quickly.

"Go," Nico coughs out the water in his lungs, "Go. Get him!"

Eric stumbles to his feet, finding the speed he just had still fresh in his muscles as he sprints down Mirror Mountain towards the Wall of Twins.

13

Branches lash at Eric like shadowy claws catching his jacket. Cold breezes rush up the mountain from the water as he runs. Each gust tightens his lung, but that doesn't stop him. It just pushes him harder. Straining lungs, the cramp ratcheting in his side, none of this mattered.

The trial, beating Mirror Eric, that's all that mattered. As Eric ran, he could hear Mirror Eric's maniacal laughter. A constant heaving laugh, forced and mocking, mixes with the crashing water following Eric down the mountain creating a discordant roar.

The mountain spirits weren't following him anymore. They stopped at the mining town. Eric doubted if he'd be able to hear them over his panting, anyway. *Are they attacking Nico right now? No! Don't think like that. Nico can handle himself. Gotta catch this guy.*

Mirror Eric shouts more taunts, more laughs. He is enjoying this. Enjoying being chased by a desperate human. Mirror Eric was a bully. No different from how Jackson held Andy's bookbag over his head and taunted him. Mirror Eric isn't holding a bookbag, no, he's holding the key to escaping Mirror Mountain. If Eric doubted that before, he didn't anymore. The wolf spirit was all the proof he needed. All this isn't natural. Ghosts. Monsters. The talking gem stone, No Face Nico, and the shack that kept appearing no matter how far they ran. *Yeah*, Eric thought, *Mirror Mountain sucks.*

Trees stopped slashing at him near the cliff's edge. The forest ended at a stone bridge. A gray flagstone bridge crossed to the other side of the mountain and looked sturdy, with bright green moss woven through the stones. Standing in the middle of the bridge was Mirror Eric. His fully formed face, Eric's face, pointing up the hill towards Eric.

Mirror Eric is smiling. At any moment, that bully was going to shout a taunt and take off running. Crossing the bridge and getting to the Wall of Twins, beating Eric. But maybe Eric could stop him the way he stops all bullies.

"Hey!" Eric shouts. "You sure got a lot to say when you're running away!"

Mirror Eric doesn't run. He leans on the side of the bridge, elbows resting in the grooves of ancient stones, watching Eric approach.

"Didn't want you to lose me." Mirror Eric sneers. "Someone as slow as you need a reminder of what he's doing."

"Caught up to you pretty quick," Eric scoffs.

"I didn't mean slow running. I meant stupid." Mirror Eric laughs. Dismissive, derisive laughter.

"Right. You know why I'm here. The wolf spirit is the proof it's all real, right?"

Mirror Eric's head tilts to one side as if he's confused by something before replying. "Did you doubt Mastermind?" Mirror Eric looks up the mountain. "Never doubt Mastermind." He says in stern admonishment.

Eric steps onto the bridge, raising his fists for a fight. "You gonna run?"

"I don't need to run." Mirror Eric turns. A soaking wet Nico crawls out of the stream.

"Now, you're done." Eric chuckles, feeling the win. Nico's here. Mirror Eric's got nowhere to go. Two against one. Mirror Eric's going to get out of the way or get thrown over the bridge. "You going to move, or are we going to move you?"

Nico walks to the bridge, stepping onto it.
"So, are you going to move both of us?" Mirror Eric laughs.
Eric takes another look at Nico, his slumped shoulders, his slack jaw. That's not his brother. That's Mirror Nico.

"Where's my brother?!" Eric shouts.

Mirror Nico shrugs, "Don't know. I've taken the river all the way down. Fastest way down." He shakes off the water, spraying cold drops like a dog.

"Now," Mirror Eric sighs, "I have to tell you one clause in the rules." He rolls his eyes with disgust.

Eric's knuckles turn white, his teeth grind as he growls, "What rules?"

"The rules of the trial." Mirror Eric grumbles, "You've lost. Once we cross this bridge, we go to the real world as you. Just smarter, better looking versions of you and your stupid brother." Mirror Eric heckles.

Mirror Nico whines, "Just tell him. Let's get this over."

Mirror Eric turns and shoos him away.

"Okay, the clause, and I'll say it slow so you can understand." Mirror Eric points up the mountain. "Go back to Mastermind. You can bargain for another chance, but the price is high, and *you* can't pay it. I'll tell the other mountain spirits to let you pass to make your trip easier. I'd rather you focus on your failure than fighting through the horde that wants to eat you." Mirror Eric chuckles.

Heavy footsteps quickly approach. Eric looks up the mountain, seeing Nico, the real Nico, emerge from the trees. Nico stops when he sees what's happening on the bridge. Eric holds up his hand, telling him to stay there. Nico does.

"What is the price?" Eric keeps looking at Nico, knowing what the last statement meant. *A high price he can't pay.* That's why Tommy is trapped here. No one else could pay for Tommy because he was alone.

Mirror Eric and Mirror Nico cross the bridge and head towards the trees. "It's different for everyone, but you're figuring it out." Mirror Eric laughs. "Maybe I'll see you around." The two Mirrors disappear into the trees.

Eric turns to Nico. His brother's eyes looking for an explanation and Eric gives him the only one he can say. "We lost."

14

Nico's face twists in confusion. "What do you mean bargain? Can't we just fight them?" He pants as he runs uphill back to Mastermind's cave. Each step is a hard climb instead of running with the flow. Now their feet are slipping and sliding as they dig into the mud and moss.

"No," Eric replies. "He said the price is high and I can't pay it."

"What's the price?" Nico asks.

Eric hesitates to answer. He doesn't want to say the words out loud. He doesn't want to make it real, but he knows he has to... not right now, "I don't know," he whispers.

The two struggle up the mountain. Trees blot out the sky, but in the breaks, Eric sees night is giving way to dawn's purple horizon. Day is coming and with it, will their Mirrors go to school? Will Dad notice anything different about them?

Eric's run slows as other thoughts boil in him. *What if Mirror Eric has the courage to ask Anna out? What if she likes him more than the real Eric? What if Mirror Eric gets to be bully buddies with Jackson? What will happen to Andy?*

"We're almost there." Nico encourages Eric as he sees the shambles of the mining town through the trees. "A little further, and we'll take a breather."

Eric picks up his pace, determined to get back before Mirror Eric screws up his last days with Anna. "I'm good. Let's keep pushing." Eric speeds up as they get to the edge of the mining town.

"No. We need a break." Nico grabs his shoulders. "Take five." Nico pants and walks with his fingers laced on top of his head. Eric recognizes this as Nico's post track race breather. He says it stretches his lungs to help him get his breath back and slow his body down after a hard run. Eric copies him.

"I'm good. Seriously. Let's go." Eric starts again. Nico pulls him back.

"You run too much, and you'll exhaust. Then I'll be carrying you." Nico takes a rhythmic breath while Eric gulps air. "Slow your breathing. Everything's going to be okay. We've got this."

"How do you know?" Eric looks away as he barks at Nico. "What if it isn't going to be okay?"

"We stay together, and we've got this," Nico responds with absolute confidence. But, Eric considers 'the price' he'll have to pay. He doesn't want to pay the price if it's what he thinks it is. Nico notices Eric staring at him. "What?"

Eric shakes his head. Slows his breathing.

They walk through the remains of the mining town. As dawn creeps through the trees, what was dusty, gray wood at night is actually a faded blonde. Maybe once this whole town was yellow. The shingles that squeak and sway and slam against wood frames aren't black like they thought, but dark gray.

Eric and Nico walk past Took's General and see the front of the building smashed in. The wolf was about to break through when

Nico did what he did. Eric blows out a relieved sigh, seeing how close they were to being… what? Being eaten? Did the wolf want to eat them? It wanted to knock them around. And the hawk that attacked Eric could have gotten his eyes but went for his back instead. Why? *Was the goal to slow me down? Does everyone lose the race, and that's why there's the clause?*

"Hey man." Nico shakes Eric. "You good?"

Eric nods and takes in a cleansing breath. "Uh, yeah. Just thinking. I'm good now. Really this time."

"Okay, stretch and then we'll get back at it. Pace ourselves this time. I don't think we're done once we get up there." Nico starts his own stretching.

Eric nods. "Yeah, you're probably right." An eagle cry breaks Eric's thoughts. Both of them look up to see the bird flying high. No monstrous qualities or amazing features, its a regular mountain eagle.

They start back up the mountain at a jog instead of a sprint. *What's going to happen when I run into Mirror Eric in town?* Will Mirror Eric give him a pat on the shoulder and say, "okay, you won?" Or will Mirror Eric fight to keep his life? *What would I do?*

He wants to say he'd fight to keep his life, but he didn't.

He didn't fight to keep Mom.

He didn't fight to keep Anna.

Is the only fight I've got in me the fight against bullies? Everything else, I just let happen. I let life happen to me like dad?

Is that who I am? A quitter? A coward? Those questions linger as they climb, jogging without breaks to the top. Eric's doubts are on the surface of his mind as he climbs into Mastermind's cavern.

15

"Why so glum, Eric?" Mastermind's voice is as chipper as ever. The pink gem flashing with each syllable.

"I'm not glum," Eric responds. He doesn't want to give Mastermind the satisfaction of knowing he's been dwelling on his personal failings.

"Good," Mastermind flickers, "let's get started, then!"

Nico slides into the cavern and stares at the glowing pink gem floating in the center of the cavern. "What?" Nico reaches out to touch it but stops himself.

"Mastermind," Eric nods towards the gem. Nico nods understanding but still watches the gem, mouth hanging open. Turning back to Mastermind, Eric continues, "Mirror Eric said there was another way?"

Mastermind chuckles, pulsing faint pink light through the cavern. Nico goes to the walls and examines the drawings. "Rules always have ways to be challenged."

"He said I need to bargain?" Eric looks at the gem. He doesn't blink. Doesn't want Mastermind to know how scared he is of what's about to happen. "I need to bargain for Nico's life?"

"Oh, no. That wouldn't be fair now, would it? No, but if one of you wants to leave, I need one of you to stay," Mastermind chirps.

"Whoever stays must commit to the next trial and that trial will not have this option. They will need to face their trial alone."

"So, whoever stays only gets one shot at their trial?" Nico asks as he comes to Eric's side.

"Yes. Those are the rules." Mastermind says. His tone is that of someone saying the most obvious thing in the world.

"Who made the rules? You?" Eric yells.

Mastermind laughs, loud and echoing. Rocks fall from the cavern and speckle the brothers' shoulders. "Oh no. Do not be ridiculous. I do not make the rules, but I ensure they are adhered to. I am Mastermind. Gamemaster makes the rules."

"I want to talk to him… her… it… whatever." Eric stumbles over the words.

Mastermind laughs, "No one talks to Gamemaster here. Gamemaster is only conversant in The Crumbling Caverns." A new door erupts up from the ground. Eric spins around and jumps away as it comes up from under his feet. The door with stalactites on it is still here. The metal door with the scales is closed again. Now this new door, the one coming up from Nico's feet, has an icon that looks like a Greek temple.

As the door stops rising, Mastermind flares, "Whoever stays, this is your trial. You must face The Temple."

"I will stay." Nico shouts.

Eric turns to him, angry that Nico answered before he had the chance. Angry that Nico is leaving him alone again.

"And so you will," Mastermind declares. Eric's face freezes in protest. "Do not worry, Eric. You will get your chance. I give you my word as Mastermind." The metal door with the balance on it, representing the Trial of Ma'at, opens slightly, letting a slice of white light into the cave.

"But first, some ground rules." Mastermind titters, "Always the rules."

Eric looks at Nico, "You're leaving me?" Fear and hurt coil on Eric's face. Abandonment wells in his eyes and burns in his cheeks.

Nico grabs Eric's shoulders, "Never. If I've gotta stay, then I'm going to be right here waiting for you. Make things right and come back. You can do anything when we do it together and we are doing this together. I'll be with you, here." Nico points to Eric's heart, "and here," he pokes Eric in the forehead, knocking him back as Nico chuckles with a playful laugh. Eric smiles too. "Use this," Nico points to Eric's head, "not those," he points to Eric's clenched fists.

"I'll come back." Eric says.

"How sweet," Mastermind chimes in. "Now, for those rules. Pay attention because these rules are critical to your successful completion of the trial."

"Rule one, you and your Mirror must pass through one of the many Wall of Twins on the mountain. Every path that leads to this cavern has a Wall of Twins. Passing through the wall will return you here as the winner." Mastermind glows a gentle pink, pulsing on each syllable.

"Rule two, you may not use any magic or magical items. Rule three, you may have no one else complete your trial for you." Mastermind's tone is sharper as he reiterates rule three. "And finally, rule four that which befalls your Mirror shall befall you in return."

"So, if I beat him up and drag him here… I'll be beat up?" Eric rolls his eyes at this last rule.

"Indeed." Mastermind says. "Are there questions? This is the one time I will ask."

Eric shakes his head and walks to the metal door he had walked through earlier. He pushes it open to blinding white nothingness.

"You will fail if you break any of the rules. Failure will result in your brother remaining here eternally and you being cast into the White Void forever," Mastermind warns. "Now enter the White Void and you will be taken home."

"I'm coming back." Eric stares at Nico.

"And I'll be here," Nico smiles. "You've got this."
Eric steps into the void. Mastermind laughs the humorless chuckle of a James Bond villain. There was something else. Eric looks back at Mastermind. There was something it didn't tell him. Too late now. Mastermind's laughter fills the void as the door slams shut.

16

The White Void evaporates like smoke, vanishing, revealing Eric's bedroom. He spins around. This is his house. He's in his room just how he left it.

I'm surprised Mirror Eric didn't wreck the place. Eric goes to his records and thumbs through the collection quickly to feel his favorites. The bent corners catch his fingers as welcome reminders that these are his records, this is his room, he is home.

Sunrise creeps through his window as a new day starts. After a night on Mirror Mountain, Eric lets the sun warm his face for a moment before he breathes a sigh of relief. But he can't shake the feeling that something is not right. Nico isn't here, but that's not the problem. Something much smaller is missing. His skateboard, the one Greenie gave him last year, isn't under his bed.

Eric runs out of his room and into the living room. He sees Nico sitting on the couch watching talk shows and eating a bag of potato chips. Crumbs tumble down his stained t-shirt. He looks like a slob.

"What are you doing here!?" Eric barks.

"Eating chips." Mirror Nico says with disinterest, "Aren't you supposed to be trapped?" He keeps his eyes on the TV and laughs at the talk show people fighting in the audience.

Eric stomps over to Mirror Nico and knocks the chip bag to the floor. "Get out of my house!"

"It's actually your dad's house," Mirror Nico corrects Eric, "and I'm here because you lost."

A chill runs down Eric's spine. "Yeah, we'll see for how long." Eric's fists tighten, and he wants to punch this Nico but doesn't. What happens to the Mirror happens to him. If he punches Mirror Nico, does it hurt his brother? Best not to find out. "Where's the other me?"

Mirror Nico shrugs. "Probably school."

"I'm suspended." Eric says through gritted teeth.

"Whatever, loser." Mirror Nico looks back at the TV with a smirk.

"Where's my dad?" Eric grabs Mirror Nico's shirt, then relaxes knowing this guy wouldn't lift a finger to do anything much less hurt his dad. That'd be too much work for this lazy jerk.
"Store." Mirror Nico points to the chip bag. "Getting more chips for me." He laughs a stuttering, eh-eh-eh noise that turns Eric's stomach.
"You're disgusting."
Eric storms out of his house, rage boiling inside him. He growls a scream at the first thing he sees. His skateboard is snapped in half on the sidewalk, "Oh, man!" Eric kneels down to the skateboard, "Why?" Picking up the pieces, "Being a jerk. That's why." He throws it down and runs towards the school.

I'm suspended. That idiot is going to get me in more trouble. The daylight and busy streets of Junction Hollow are a welcome difference from the isolation and gloom of Mirror Mountain. He runs to school, realizing he should have checked the time before he left the house.

To the east of town, the top of Mirror Mountain is obscured by clouds. It almost looks like it's smoking. *Has Nico's trial started? Probably not.* Mastermind said Eric needed to succeed to release the keys. *What did that mean?*

What if I lose again? What if I can't beat my Mirror? Eric's mind races with the possibilities as he nears school. Can I do this alone? He's so lost in thought that he doesn't see the other Eric until it's too late.

The two Erics collide and tumble to the ground. Eric's backpack goes flying and if it had any books, they would have spilled, but Eric never put much mind to school and neither does his Mirror. "You again!" Mirror Eric snarls as he jumps up.

"What are you doing here?" Eric scrambles to his feet and looks around. From here, Eric can see the students in the hallways of Junction Hollow Middle. The bells have rung to get everyone to class.

"I'm going to school." Mirror Eric says with a smirk. "Unlike you, I'm not suspended."

"Of course you are!" Eric mutters. "They'll all think you're me! You idiot."
"I'm you, so you are an idiot too. And you're a coward." Mirror Eric steps forward and shoves Eric in the chest. "A chicken."

Eric stumbles back but catches himself. He's not going to back down this time. As Mirror Eric comes close to push again, Eric shoves him back and instantly falls backward at the same time. Suddenly Mastermind's words come back to him… whatever is done to his Mirror shall be returned to him.

Mirror Eric sees Eric fall down from his own push and laughs. "Oh, that's too funny." He stands back up. "So, I can push you, but you can't push me? I bet you can't do anything to me… or I bet anything you do to me happens to you."

Eric's eyes narrow as he snarls. "For now."

"Well, better get to school. Don't want to be late." Mirror Eric winks. "Oh, and I'll make sure to say hi to Anna for you." He laughs.

Eric's fists tighten again. He wants to pass his fist right through his Mirror's teeth but knows that will just hurt him. *Might be worth it? No. Probably not.* Mirror Eric trots off, almost skipping in glee as Eric turns and punches a wall in frustration. His hand instantly screams in agony and Eric realizes immediately that didn't help anything.

Mirror Eric goes in school, shoving his way through the crowded hallway. Eric watches. Helpless as his evil twin takes over his life.

17

Eric storms away from the school. Only a few days left before Anna leaves, a week before Andy, and what's Mirror Eric going to do? He's going to ruin that time. He's going to make it so they leave hating Eric and worst of all, Mirror Eric isn't going to do anything to make them stay.

And what's going to happen when Mr. Henderson sees him? Double suspension? Expulsion?

There's nothing Eric can do about it. Mirror Eric is doing what he wants. The question is, what will Eric do now?

He can't go home. His dad will be suspicious if two Erics show up. *But what about Mirror Nico? Is Dad in danger?* Eric doesn't think so. Mirror Nico is lazy and probably wouldn't get off the couch. He laughs at the thought of Mirror Nico getting up to get himself more chips.

Nico is always doing something. Always hustling. Always protesting or working or building or learning. Always moving and making things move.

Mirror Eric's strut and swagger, Mirror Nico's sloth, their Mirrors are the opposite of them. And that opposite is pretending to be Eric today. "Well, I can't just stand here." Eric looks around, seeing the streets empty as the school bell rings, calling everyone to their seats.

"Where can I disappear for a few hours?" Eric looks around

when an idea hits him. He spots the clock tower at the center of town. The clock tower above the Junction Hollow Public Library. "Perfect." He walks to the library. Nobody would question him being there. *I'm just doing research.*

Another idea hits him: *maybe I can find information about Mirror Mountain.* He might figure out what's going on with all the strange stuff on that mountain while he waits for school to end. Someone had to have encountered the Wall of Twins or Mastermind before now. If they did, there'd be an article or book about it. He can't be the first person to face the Trial of Ma'at…can he?
***

Junction Hollow Public Library's bookshelves towered over Eric with ladders on wheels at the end of each aisle. Each shelf was white where the paint hadn't chipped off. Like everything in Junction Hollow, the library was old and needed a fresh coat of paint, among other repairs. The tables wobbled, the chairs squeak, and the books cracked but not from being broken. In fact, the only thing in this library that wasn't broken were the books. Eric knew why. No one came to the library anymore. These books were unused, unloved. The town had abandoned it like everything else, like everyone else.

In the local history section, one book stood out on the shelf: Cryptids of Junction Hollow. On the cover was a drawing of a wolf encased in a thick turtle shell. Eric sucks back a shriek at the sight. He covers his mouth, pressing the scream deeper into himself.

Eric pulls the book and sits at one of the least wobbly tables. He flips through pages and pages of stories where unknown creatures are spotted around Junction Hollow. Some creatures would terrorize the town, some were symbols foretelling a coming disaster, like when the two major mine shafts collapsed in 1935.
The creatures described in this book were each representation of

other animals smashed together. One was a giant hawk that looked like a bear called a One Nose Chimera. Eric shrugs his shoulder and winces at the sharp pain from the cuts on his back. The next page is a wolf with a hard, impenetrable shell called an Iron Back Razor Tooth. Eric nods at the name, finding it very fitting.

Eric stops flipping when he sees a picture of a person without a face. His finger jumps to the name on the page, Doppelgänger. "That's it."
He whispers as he reads the entry aloud, "Doppelgangers are spirits that manifest into the form of a person or animal they wish to impersonate. Impersonation leads to replacement of the person or animal, as the Doppelgänger is possessive and superstitious."

Eric looks up from the book, processing the information. He suddenly realizes how silent the library is with no one in it. No foot steps or pages flipping. No seats creaking or carts rattling. *Where's the librarian?* He wonders as he settles in and continues reading.

"While many doppelgangers are simple spirits with an identity crisis, some are spirits that invert their target's personality. These Doppelgangers are known as Flipman. The name refers to how they flip the person they are impersonating. Flipman takes pleasure in destroying the lives of their targets and does not forget their true nature. Once a Flipman takes hold, they ruin their target's life and then leave back to their source in the woods of Mirror Mountain."

Eric sighs, *yeah that sounds about right. Mirror Eric is a Flipman.*

Throughout the cryptid descriptions, another book is often referenced: Junk Hole: The Hidden History of Junction Hollow. Eric wonders if this book is in the library. A quick search on the computer shows it is.

Following the decimal system, Eric finds the book and pulls

it from the shelf. It's filled with yellowed pages, smelling like old newspapers and wet basements. When he opens it, the spine crackles a gleeful welcome.

An inscription on the title page reads. *To the town of Junction Hollow. Let this be your reminder of why. Sincerely, — RM.* Eric flips back to the cover to see the author, Luis Elderman. Who is *RM?* Deep scars from the pen and angry, scraggling lines for the signature tell Eric, RM was no friend of Junction Hollow. Eric digs into the book, turning the pages gently to avoid ripping the ancient paper. He stops on the copyright page and sees the book's copyright date is June 6, 1968.

The book is a collection of diary entries, newspaper articles, and personal accounts of the founding fathers and mothers of Junction Hollow. Letters and notes from 1860 to 1968… 108 years to the date.

The first entry is dated June 6th, 1860. It's a letter from a man named William to his wife, Caroline. William worked at the mining company and was searching for his fortune in gold. He wrote about how strange he found this place, without trees or wildlife. Describing it as more of a swamp than forest. But then he noticed something else in the distance. "A mirror shimmering off the horizon."

As Eric flips through the rest of the book, he sees this description repeated by other diary entries and personal accounts. *What does that mean? A mirror shimmering off the horizon?*

On the last entry, dated June 6, 1968, there's an article written by a woman named Maelynne who talked about her son, Daniel Newman. She said that she had always known something was different about him. He never fit in with the other kids and loved to stay out in the woods on his own.

On June 6, when Daniel disappeared, she realized how special he really was. She described hearing a strange sound coming from above Mirror Mountain and found Daniel staring up at the moon. He turned to her and said, "The time has come."

After that, Daniel was never the same. He stopped going to school and barely left the house. He wouldn't do anything else except write. He wrote all day and into the night. But Maelynne never read his work. She wrote it was for him and him alone.

Until now.

Maelynne wrote she found this book after Daniel's disappearance and that it was his legacy. She hoped it will help the townspeople remember what happened and why they should never forget. Eric flips the last page, then flips back.

"What was in the book?" Eric flips quickly back through the last pages, forgetting about their frailty. He looks for any sign of a title or what was in the book, but finds nothing. "Ugh… cliffhanger? Really?"

"Shhh!" comes from behind a bookshelf in a hissing signal that he is not alone. The librarian's chair creaks as she shifts. Eric shushes himself and takes a deep sigh of relief that someone else is in the building. The ticking clock takes over the silence of the library again as Eric continues to flip through the pages.

A familiar symbol stops him: The Eye of Horus. On the inside cover of the book, right where the binding meets the front cover, he sees this same symbol scratched in so many times it's almost unrecognizable. How did he miss this? He recognizes the symbol from his world history class, but what is it doing in this book?

Eric's mind goes back to the missing kid. The kid mentioned at the end of the book. *Did he go up Mirror Mountain? Was he the Mirror or the real kid? Maybe there was a news article about this missing boy?* Eric looks at the computers and takes his books.

Opening his search engine, Eric types in, "Daniel Newman missing 1968." He clicks SEARCH. The computer thinks about his question. As it thinks, an older lady glares at him from over her glasses. Her tight gray perm and winged gold rim glasses on a beaded chain remind him of an angry librarian from TV. Her furrowed brow and unblinking stare emphasize the point.

Search results return with a news article from a week after June 6, 1968. The headline reads, Missing Boy Found. The photo under the headline shows a bunch of men huddled around the boy, who is wrapped in a blanket. Reading further, "Miners find the missing boy, Daniel Newman, stuck in a hole inside Mine Entrance 3 on Mirror Mountain. The boy said he fell while exploring the mine." Eric reads on, skimming the news about the heroism of the miners and the dangers of playing in active mines. Looking back at the picture, Eric notices something in Daniel's hand. Eric zooms in to the picture, seeing a symbol. He looks closer, the old photograph pixelating to blurs. As Eric squints and tilts his head, he can make out the teeth of a key on one side of Daniel's hand. On the other side is a carving Eric recognizes.

"Oh, crap!" He springs back away from the monitor.

"Shhhh!" the librarian hisses. She stomps over and glowers at him. "Young man, a library is a place of quiet and civility. Not a place for your profanity!"

Eric looks at her, confused. He wonders what profanity she's talking about? Crap?

"Shouldn't you be in school?" The librarian asks, her beady eyes narrowing.

"I, um," Eric starts, but a lie doesn't come fast enough.

"Well?" The librarian taps her foot.

"I'm doing research for a school project." He holds up the books as evidence.

"Unlikely!" the librarian barks. "You are cutting school and think you can hide here! Well, the library isn't just a place of fun and games where you can party all day!"

While partying at the library sounds very contradictory to Eric, he doesn't respond. Excuses and explanations try to form in his mind, but they don't come together fast enough. He'd never been a good liar, but the school bell sounds up the street and pivots his thoughts to a more pressing concern.
School is out.
Eric's Mirror is loose on Junction Hollow again. Eric has to catch him before anything else is ruined. Standing up to leave, the librarian grabs his arm.

"Not so fast." She snarls. "You can't just cut school and get away with it. Let's give your parents a call to see if they know where you've been today. Yes?" She smiles a gotcha grin.

Eric doesn't want to explain all this to his dad. Even he doesn't believe it and he's living it. There's no way his dad would believe him. Eric tugs his arm free from the librarian's grip and bolts for the door.

"Hey! Come back here! You have to checkout those books!" The librarian shouts, but Eric is already out the door with his two books pressed to his chest.

"I'll bring them back!" He shouts back to her as he hustles towards the school. Turning through some back streets, none of which are too long in Junction Hollow, he comes out to the school soccer field. Running across it, he takes cover by some bushes at the edge of the field.

Eric peeks over the bushes and sees Andy stumble out from a cluster of kids leaving the school like he was ejected from the crowd. He tumbles to the pavement, chin bounces off the asphalt, leaving slashes of scrapes.

"Jackson?" Eric curls his fist, but it's not Jackson behind Andy. It's him. Mirror Eric steps out of the mass of people leaving school and stands over Andy. He laughs and points as others gather around to see what's going on. Everyone loves seeing a fight.

Andy crawls away from Mirror Eric. "Why?" Andy cries. "What did I do?"

"You were born a loser." Mirror Eric snarls and stomps Andy's book bag with a plastic and metal crunch. Andy screams and reaches for his backpack, but Mirror Eric kicks the backpack away.

Eric knows that was Andy's drone. The one Andy made with spare parts his dad found around the factory before he was fired. Anger boils up in Eric as he steps up to do what he does best: fight bullies.

18

CRACK!

Eric drops into the bushes. White dots pop in his vision. Trembling pain explodes out from his jaw. He rolls out of the bushes to see what hit him. Mirror Eric is rolling on the ground under the tall, beautiful Anna. Her fist still hangs in the air. She slowly retracts it, her shoulders heaving with anger.

"What's wrong with you!?" Anna screams at Mirror Eric. "You've been acting a fool all day, Eric! Cut it out!" She stomps over to Andy and pulls him up easily. He looks like an elementary school kid beside her. She's so tall and Andy is so small. Anna picks up his book bag and hands it to him. He takes it and feels all the broken parts. Andy presses the bookbag to his chest and lets his tears fall.

Mirror Eric laughs. "Is that all you've got?"

In the bushes, Eric can feel his lip swelling, his jaw tightening and hopes that is all she's got.

Mirror Eric staggers up and pulls Anna's arm while she helps Andy. Eric winces, knowing that was an incredibly stupid thing to do. Anna grabs Mirror Eric's wrist and throws him over her shoulder. The crushing landing blasts through both Eric's shoulders and back. It drops him to the ground again; the impact taking his air, leaving him with black spots bursting where the white ones just were.

Eric groans and rolls in pain.

Anna is comforting Andy and guiding him away from Mirror Eric. They're heading his way. He rolls into the bushes, down the hill where they won't see him. As they walk past, Eric wants to call out to them, but he can't breathe from that throw, much less talk.

"Why'd he do that?" Andy cries.

"He's changing. Just like everyone else around here…" Anna sighs.

Eric looks to Mirror Eric from the bushes and sees the crowd disperse. Struggling to his feet, Eric heads towards his Flipman, his Doppelgänger still rolling and laughing in the street.

"What the heck was that?" Eric yells.

"A little fun." Mirror Eric rolls to his knees and stands. He points to Eric's face. "It was worth it." Mirror Eric laughs.

Eric holds his face, his fingers tracing over the lump in his lip, the bump growing on his jawbone. "What is wrong with you? Why are you doing this?"

"Being nice is so boring." Mirror Eric shrugs.

"So, you decide to just be a jerk instead?" Eric spits blood on the ground. Inside his mouth, he can feel where he bit his cheek from Anna's punch. The copper taste fills his mouth again, and he spits it out.

"I'm the opposite of you." Mirror Eric laughs and spits blood, too. "I've gotta be me. And it's good to be bad." Mirror Eric smiles and draws out the last word. He winks at Eric as if begging for a slap, a punch.

Eric knows that's what he wants and wants to give it to Mirror Eric, but Nico's words come back. *Use your head.* Taking a deep breath, Eric steps back away from his evil twin and walks off into Junction Hollow. Eric expects his Mirror to shout at him, to threaten him, but it doesn't say anything. Just walks away.

Did Mirror Eric ruin my chances with Anna? Does it matter? She's moving away, anyway. Eric shakes the thought away. *Of course it matters.* He can't let her leave Junction Hollow thinking he is such a jerk.

Eric runs to Anna's house. It is a tall, beautiful house. It matches her. The red shutters and white siding of the house match the red for sale sign swinging from the white post in her front yard. Three signs just like it line the road. Those houses are abandoned because no one would buy them. Is Anna's house headed for the same fate? He runs up the steps to her porch and knocks hard on her red front door.

The door swings open. Anna's puffy wet cheeks and red eyes meet Eric's. She pushes the door hard to slam it. He puts his hand on the door. Her eyes sharpen. He talks fast to avoid getting a black eye to match his fat lip.

"Wait!" Eric pleads. "I can explain."

"Go ahead." She pushes on the door again to close it. Eric lightly pushes back, holding up his other hand in a peace offering.

"That wasn't me." he says, "It's," he thinks of what to say, "it's a long story."

"I don't have time for your stories, Eric." Anna's voice cracks. Her eyes are blotshot and streaked with dark red lines. He searched in those eyes for a way to fix things, but all he found was pain and disappointment.

"I know." Eric nods his head. "But I promise, it's—"

"No." Anna shakes her head. "I was stupid. I should have seen this. Everyone changes here. Everyone gets like Jackson. Angry. I'm angry. You're angry. My dad was right." Anna's eyes stab at Eric. Her mouth curls in disgust. "Everything's rotting here in Junk Hole. Even good people are rotting into bad people." She slams the door.

Eric stands there listening to her footsteps quickly stomp upstairs as she cries. "Crap." he whispers. "Now what?" *Andy?* Eric wonders if he'd have better luck with Andy. *Andy believes in aliens and ghosts, so maybe I can start there. Start with the truth.*

Eric runs to Andy's house a few blocks up. The sun is hiding behind Mirror Mountain as the afternoon hours tick away. Mastermind's laughing erupts in Erici's mind. Why did Mastermind laugh like that? Are there more rules that he didn't tell me? *Is there a time limit for this trial? Will Nico face the consequences of me being too slow?* Eric runs up the steps of Andy's porch and bangs on the door. "Andy! Come on, man, I need to talk to you!"

Two eyes, encased in thick black-rimmed glasses, peek around the front window's curtain. "Go away!" Andy screams through the closed window.

"That wasn't me, it was an alien!" Eric shouts.

The eyes at the curtain narrow in silent consideration. Behind Eric, a kid rides by on their bike. She had playing cards clicking against her tire spokes. Another kid up the street was throwing a football to a friend and shouting. A man with a scraggly black beard and gray hoodie was walking on the other side of the street. Andy's answer took forever, but Eric knew he couldn't pressure him. Andy never performed under pressure.

"Prove it." Andy says quietly.

"I went up Mirror Mountain, and that thing came down instead of me," Eric whispers so people around by can't hear his crazy story. "Its like an alien or ghost or something. I need your help."

Andy steps back from the window, and a second later, he opens the door. His eyes widen at Eric's face, but he doesn't ask about his fat lip. "So? Why would I help you after all the crud you did today? Just cause you're made we're leaving, you gotta be like a jerk." Eric shook his head. "It's not like that. Look, I can prove it. The other me is at my house right now. Just come with me. I'll show you." Eric motions for Andy to follow.

Andy eyes Eric suspiciously. "How do I know you're not the alien?" Andy asks.

Eric nods, realizing its a very obvious question he should have prepared for. "Um… I don't know. Come with me, please?" He adds quietly, hoping a plea to Andy's fear of alien invasions will be enough to sway him. "If you don't help me, then who knows how many more are coming, right?"

Andy sighs. His head bobbles in agreement. "Alright, let's go."

Eric smiles and rushes up the street before Andy can change his mind. He knows he should probably be more careful. But what choice does he have? He needs Andy's help to fix this mess.

As they approach Eric's house, Andy slows down and starts to look around nervously. "It looks normal." he says skeptically.

"Yeah, this is my real house," Eric whispers and ducks down to stay under the line of windows around his house. Like many of the cookie cutter houses in the area of Junction Hollow known as "New Town," Eric's house was a rancher with many windows surrounding the house. *Sunlight keeps you positive,* Eric's mom used to say. She loved all the windows, but now, Eric just saw them as obstacles. *I'm positive we're going to be seen.* He laughs.

Keeping low, Eric waves for Andy to follow, and Andy does. Ducking down and crawling with Eric, they both sit under Eric's bedroom window. "This is my room."

"I know." Andy says with a no-duh face.

Eric pops his head up slowly to look in the window. Mirror Eric is in there, drawing on the walls with black marker. "See? See?"

Andy's eyes widen, and he nods. "Okay, now what?" Andy asks quietly. "How do I know that's the alien, and you're the real you?"

"Would I draw on my walls?" Eric reads the writing. "You think I'd write 'Eric's a dork'?" Eric sighs, hoping Andy knows that he'd be more creative than that.

Andy nods in agreement. "You'd write something about Anna."

Eric leans away from Andy. *I'd write about her eyes.* "No," he shakes away the thought, remembering Anna's expression of disgust when he came to her door. There's no chance those eyes will ever smile his way again. "Stay focused."

Andy peeks again. Dropping back quickly, "So, I believe you. Something's weird. What do we do now?"

"I need you to talk to Anna for me." Eric whispers, "She won't listen to me, but she might listen to you. You can make her believe me, right?"

Andy sighs and nods his head. "Yeah, I can try."

They crawl back to the sidewalk and slide behind the tree Eric used to climb when he was little. Andy glances back, checking if Mirror Eric saw them, but he didn't.

"Hey!" Mirror Nico yells from the front porch. "Dad, there's a weird kid creeping around our house!" Mirror Nico smiles at Eric.

"Run!" Eric says, pulling Andy's arm.

19

"Hey!" Eric's dad yells but doesn't chase.

Andy runs as fast as his stick thin legs will take him. Eric keeps pace. "We've got this." He channels Nico, saying what he thinks Nico would tell him. "He's not going to catch us." Eric says, but he doesn't sound very convincing. "He's not chasing us but keep running. If we stop running," Eric pants, "he might change his mind."

"We're going to have to face him, eventually." Andy says, out of breath as he slows down to a jog. Eric's dad is still on the porch but hardly visible from here.

"I know." Eric sighs and stops running. He walks with his fingers laced atop his head, just like Nico does, to catch his breath.

"Now what?" Andy gasps.

Suddenly, the exhaustion of running and hiding for 24-hours straight crashes over Eric. His mind and muscles swim with a level of tiredness he's never felt before. "I think I need a break." Eric wonders, *do the rules allow a break? Is Nico okay? Maybe a break isn't in the cards.* "No, no. I'm okay to keep going."

"No. You're not." Andy says, reaching to hold Eric up. "You're about to pass out. When's the last time you slept?"

"I guess…" Eric thinks hard. Harder than it should take, but a tired mind runs slow. "Two days ago?"

"Let's go to my house. You can crash there. I'll sneak you in around back." Andy waves Eric forward. Eric's legs slowly grind into motion as he hopes a little rest won't doom Nico… or him.

A few minutes later, they're back at Andy's house. Andy goes in the front door and chats with his parents. Eric slumps beside a bush under Andy's window and waits. Andy's house is the same rancher as Eric's. The bedroom window is the same. Déjà vu hits Eric as he rests his eyes, rubs his numb legs. Eric's head swims. His eyes close without his permission.

***

"Eric!" Andy stage whispers.

No response.
Did the alien get him? Andy pokes his head further out the window. *What planet did they come from? Why are they here? Why does it look like Eric?* Thoughts sprinted through Andy's head as fast as he wished he could run.

Andy wasn't the kid who was a superhero because of cool powers. He would be a hero like Tony Stark. His brains were his superpower. Not running like Eric or fighting like Anna.

"Eric?" Andy whispers again. No response. He picks up his latest weapon design from his desk–a sonic grenade and a pair of headphones. Andy thinks, *if the aliens are here, maybe this will drive them away.* He shakes the circuit board, wires, and speaker in his hand. *Maybe they have super sensitive ears, and this will make their heads explode?* Andy didn't want that. Or the mess that would bring. His sonic grenade was a re-engineered smoke alarm, amplified and triggered by a button he added on his circuit board.

Going outside, Andy put on the headphones and nervously looked around. "Eric?" He asked again as he made his way to his window. *What if they ate Eric? What if they're going to eat me? How did Invasion of the Body Snatchers work? That's what this looks like, pod people...*

Under Andy's window, Eric sleeps. Checking around him, Andy doesn't see any pod people or pods, just muddy footprints. Maybe Eric was pacing before he fell asleep? A loud cheer from the TV room breaks his attention and Andy looks back towards his door, thinking, *Mom and Dad are watching that stupid singing game show. I gotta be quiet.*

When Andy comes out his front door, he stops. His heart sinks with a hard swallow. A man in a hoodie, with a black beard, is staring at his backyard. Andy wonders if the man's casing out his house, getting ready to break in and steal all their stuff just like he's heard in his mom's true crime podcasts. Or maybe the man's just homeless and dirty? Their eyes meet and the man hurries down the street, but Andy notices his muddy shoes and how the man's hands are shoved in his pockets.

The man turns down the street and keeps walking. *All clear,* Andy thinks, *time for Operation Sandman.* Reading gave Andy all the ideas of adventure and excitement he'd love to have in his life. There was always Mission This, or Operation That, all to break the boredom of watching TV with his parents and hiding from the world with them on weeknights. They just wanted to watch TV after work. Andy wanted to adventure and now he had the chance.

Operation Sandman is getting Eric in the house unnoticed. But Andy, being the computer and reading type, not the athletic type, couldn't carry him. Instead, Andy went to the garden shed, got a wheelbarrow and pushed Eric into the barrow. Eric lay twisted and bent in uncomfortable poses as the wheelbarrow bounced through the muddy yard.

A sharp CRACK stops Andy from pushing. He rolls the wheelbarrow back and sees that he ran over a black pen cap. The plastic cap snapped under the weight of the Eric filled wheelbarrow. *Eric must have dropped that from his pocket.*

Hitting a deep hole in the yard, the wheelbarrow jerks, almost falls. Andy stabilizes it in time, but not before two books tumble out of Eric's jacket onto the grass. He picks them up and tosses them on Eric.
Andy wheels him inside. His mom and dad are trapped in the grip of who is going to win the microphone tonight when one of Eric's books slides off him and hits the floor with a floomp. Andy freezes. His parents don't move. Too enthralled by the final judge's decision. He grabs the book and rushes away.

Getting through his door isn't easy, but Andy made it with slamming Eric's head into the wall only one or two times. Once inside, Andy closes the door and dumps Eric out of the wheelbarrow and onto his bed. But Eric slides off and smacks his head again, this time on the floor. Andy winces as drool pools around Eric's cheek.

"Sorry Eric." Andy goes to lift him, but can't. He makes a bed on the floor, and rolls Eric onto it.

The sonic grenade is placed back on Andy's desk. He looks at the row of weapons. The High Pressure Glue Gun, the Marble Slick Trap, and his LED Net were all ready to use for an alien invasion like this. But, like any glorious hero, Andy knows he can't just barge in spraying glue everywhere. He needs a plan and to build a plan; he needs to understand the enemy.

Andy picks up Eric's books and smiles. *Time to use my ultimate weapon, literacy!*

***

Eric sleeps the sleep of a man whose body says no more. Marathon runners, soldiers, emergency responders know this sleep. It is the sleep where the body and mind are done. They need to just sit in the motionless dark and recharge.

Hours pass until Eric comes back to the world. His eyes open to see Andy's silhouette. The computer monitor light around Andy is blinding in the darkroom. There's a noise, some mechanical whirring. Eric scans the room and finds the source, a 3D printer busily stacking melted plastic, making something.

"Andy?" Eric *says*.

"Yeah." Andy turns in his chair. His thick glasses amplifying the monitor light behind him. "Oh! Eric. I see you're awake." Andy pushes a glass of water towards Eric. "Here. You need to hydrate." A bottle of orange sports drink follows the water. "Oh, wow, you were not kidding about the weird stuff going on!"

Andy waves Eric to the desk with a gleeful smile. Checking his legs, Eric finds they can support him a little longer as he walks over and sits beside Andy.

"Okay, I found your books." Andy holds up the books Eric borrowed from the library. "And I found your notes." Andy opens the Junction Hollow history book and points to handwritten passages in the margins of the pages.

"Wait." Eric looks at the page. "I didn't write any notes." Eric reads the first note Andy points to. "Not Daniel, Danny. No one called him Daniel." The note references Daniel Newman, the kid who disappeared, but Eric recognizes the handwriting. It is his. "That's my handwriting, but I don't remember writing that?" Eric shakes his head.

Andy sucks in a deep breath and beams in excitement. Eric leans back, waiting for Andy's head to burst. "Oh man! That's sooo cool!" Andy flips further back in the book. "I thought it was you because someone just wrote this." He stops on a page with freshly smeared black ink. The note reads, "When the keys are released, Gamemaster is in play. Beware Gamemaster. Beware Toelm. Neither to be trusted."

"That wasn't there earlier." Eric says. It's the page that ends with mentioning Daniel Newman's book. He looked at that page several times and saw no notes like this.

"Oh, man! Operation Mysterious Notes is afoot!" Andy nods and turns to his computer. He clicks the mouse to a web browser tab and points to a passage of text.
Eric reads the web page header and snickers with a laugh. "Ghost Hunters Association of West Central State? Couldn't come up with a shorter name?"

Andy waves away the comment. "The G.H.A.W.C.S., or g-hawks, as I call them, are a serious organization. Look at this." Andy taps the screen.

"Mysterious disappearance cycles of mountain towns." Eric reads about how every 53.5 years, people start disappearing from Junction Hollow. Many of the people are found a few days later, but often their family and friends say those people are different. Somehow changed. They didn't always come back right away. Once, someone returned many weeks later. Eric skims for the name of who returned, but he knows. His eyes hit the name and stop. Daniel Newman.

"But it's not aliens." Andy points out. "It's like spirits or something." He says, disappointed. Eric nods as he keeps reading the article. "Looks like a curse or something," Andy says and points to another picture, this one the Eye of Horus. "There was an archeology dig site where—"

"People found Egyptian artifacts." Eric says. The carving on the door handle, the Trial of Ma'at. The Eye of Horus. These are symbols from Egypt, but how'd they get here in West Virginia?

"Yeah." Andy laughs. "So, I'm thinking that there's something like the mummy's curse going on here, but instead of being like radioactive chemicals, it's actually a curse." Andy nods slowly. "Not gonna lie. I was hoping for aliens, but Operation Mummy's Curse still sounds awesome."

Eric pats Andy's shoulder and wonders how many operations this makes now. Andy winces at being touched. Eric pulls his hand back, remembering his Mirror pushing Andy down. "Sorry. I didn't mean to—"

"I know it wasn't you. Now we gotta convince Anna that." Andy's eyes grow to match what he knows will be a herculean task.

The whirring 3D printer keeps going while Eric and Andy consider the conversation with Anna.

"Making a new drone?" Eric remembers the one smashed in the book bag. Andy shakes his head.

"No, I saw this photo here about these stick bundles that look like people." Andy scrolls to the image, and Eric gasps in recognition. "You saw these? I mean, you saw these outside the book?" Andy points to a yellow sticky note in the Cryptids of Junction Hollow and flips to the page it marks. There, the stick figures are seen hanging between trees.

Eric nods and flashes back to pushing through the dangling stick figures on Mirror Mountain. What he'd later know was the Wall of Twins.

"Well, it sounded like they were important, so I'm printing a few." Andy taps the yellow sticky note. In bold letters, it reads '*Important*,' written in Eric's handwriting. "I extrapolated a 3D image from all these 2D photos. Simple stuff really." Andy shrugs.

"What are we going to do with them?" Eric asks.

Andy smiles, "I don't know, but I know someone who lives in Junction Hollow that can probably help."

"Who?" Eric squints to see Andy's wild smile. A bad idea is brewing behind those glasses. There was a time when Andy was a wellspring of bad ideas. Eric remembers the old days when Andy was quite the troublemaker. Not that he tried to be a problem, not that he tried to break things or start fires, but Andy was always curious. That curiosity often led to experiments, and those experiments often led to disasters. *Are we heading towards disaster?*

Andy clicks on another tab, opening a picture of an old man working in his garden appears. The caption under the picture reads: "'Some things never change in Junction Hollow', says Mr. Daniel Newman."

"Daniel Newman is still alive and still in Junction Hollow." Andy beams.

Eric nods, smiles slowly, and agrees. *If anyone knows what's going on… it's him.*

20

Andy told his parents he was sick and needed to stay home from school today. They did the normal checks, felt his head, cheeks, and neck for signs of fever. Clammy skin. Hot temperature. And they found all those things along with sniffles. They granted Andy a sick day to recover.

But Andy was not sick. He manufactured all the symptoms with simple tools like heating pads, spicy chicken vindaloo and frozen water in a spray bottle. Last night, Eric and Andy hatched the plan to stay home from school and get into some trouble. While they said *trouble* in a joking way, they didn't know how right they would be, and not the fun trouble either. The run for your life trouble. But before they could get to that, Eric had to wait in the closet while Andy had to wait in his bed.

After Andy's parents left for work, the boys waste no time getting out the door to find Daniel Newman. Like all things in the modern world, Daniel Newman's address was online and easy to find for those who know how to look. Andy rode his bike, Eric rode on the back bars. They swerved and bumped along back alleys to avoid questions about why they weren't in school.

They stop at Livingston Street. On one side of the street was green grass, freshly mowed and manicured. On the other was Old Town, crumbled brown grass, shaggy and forgotten.

Old Town was the last section of Junction Hollow built during the mining days. Many of the houses were built for the miners and then owned by the mining company. Miners would rent the house, rent the tools, rent the ability to work and always get paid just a little less than they owed the mining company. Eric had learned about the questionable business practices of the old mining company Boyers Mining in history class. They put children younger than him to work in deadly tunnels that could explode with methane at any moment. The money was enough to keep the families here, enough to build hope that one day they could make more money than they owed.

But now, these houses are abandoned just like everything else in Junction Hollow.

Old Town had its own cookie cutter style house, except for less variation. Every house in Old Town looked like two houses piled on each other. The bottom of every house was pale olive, usually faded with age, with one window over the kitchen sink and another in the first floor living room.

On top of the rancher was a smaller house that was faded yellow with olive trim. It looked like a single bedroom, with a window on top of the rancher. Eric always thought they looked like shacks on top of a real house.

He never went into Old Town, had no need. New Town is closer to the factory and the newer parts of town. All the modern life in Junction Hallow fled Old Town for New Town. Now life flees New Town. Like a sinking ship, the rats escaped the lower decks, Old Town, and now are abandoning the main deck, New Town.

Andy drifts on his bike down Livingston St, stopping at the mailbox labeled Newman. The letters were faded with the first three, chipped away by time and indifference. Both boys look slowly up the wild overgrown yard. Their eyes follow the broken and blackened concrete path to the front porch, which sags and scowls with jagged latticework. A sign by the door reads: "No Solicitors, No Well Wishers and No One Else. Go away!"

"Looks friendly." Andy shrugs.

Eric climbs down and leads the way. Andy leans his bike against the mailbox, checking the street to see if anyone will mess with it. Most of the houses are boarded-up. In Junction Hollow that means abandoned. If a house couldn't sell when the family had to move, the real estate company would eventually board it up to keep away any troublemakers. Today, the only troublemakers left in Junction Hollow were Andy and Eric.

Andy chuckles, thinking about how this town will soon be a ghost town, and then remembers Mirror Eric and Mirror Nico. He stops laughing and wonders if the town already is populated by more ghosts than people.

Eric pushes the doorbell. No sound. He listens for any movement as Andy joins him on the porch. Eric wonders, *when was the last time Newman mowed the lawn?* Looking to the other houses, all over grown probably with snakes enjoying the cover of long grass, *a lawn mowing business would be good money here in Old Town. If these people had any money or if people lived in these houses.*

"Go away is clearly on the door!" A man yells from inside the house. His voice is horse and rough. A cough follows.

"We're looking for Daniel Newman about a key he found." Eric shouts back.

Fast footsteps come to the door, and it swings open just as fast. A skeletal man with stringy white hair thrusts his head out the door. "Who sent you?" Behind the door, Eric can see the dirty, used-to-be-white, bathrobe Newman is wearing over a once upon a time white sleeveless shirt and long pale blue pajama pants.

"I just have some questions," Eric shakes his head and looks Daniel in the eyes, "I'm," he juggles his hands, not sure how to say it, "I'm on trial…?"

Daniel nods and opens the door wider. "Yes, well, come in. Come in. Get out of the cold."

Eric glances at Andy, questioning. *Cold? It's easily 75 out here.* Eric dismisses the comment, assuming old people get cold easily. They both go inside as Daniel closes the door.

CLICK! Daniel locks the deadbolt with a key after they come inside. He drops the key in his robe pocket.

"Take a seat." Daniel flicks his hand at the couch, covered in wiry cat hair. Andy looks for cats. None to be seen. Or heard. Eric sits as Daniel slowly lowers himself into a recliner. His old knees pop and creak in protest as he sits. "So, it is time for another trial? Another passing." Daniel motions to the sky and arcs his hand.

"You had the key in a picture I saw. When the miners found you in the cave." Eric explains.

"Yes, yes… the cave," Daniel looks at Andy, "Did you go together?"

"I went with my brother." Eric answers, "He's still in the cave waiting for me to finish my trial. I had to race my Mirror down the mountain. He won." Eric looks to the floor.

Daniel nods, "And so, the keys have not been released yet?"

Eric shakes his head, "Mastermind—"

"Ahhhh… Mastermind." Daniel looks to the sky again, his memories taking him away from the dirty living room. Stacks of old magazines and piles of soda cans create narrow paths leading from the recliner to the kitchen, the kitchen to the back rooms. Another path splits off to stairs across the room. "So, you are at the beginning." He nods.

Eric agrees.

Andy watches Daniel closely and wonders, *where are the cats? All this cat hair came from somewhere. What kind of cats have such wiry hair? Short brown wiry hair?*

"Why did you come?" Daniel asks.

Eric leans forward. "How do I stop my Mirror?" The direct question surprises Daniel, who sits back as if it pushed him deeper in his chair. Then, Daniel laughs like gravel scraping against sand-paper.

"Mastermind told you that. It is the rules." Daniel says and nods solemnly.

Eric sighs in exasperation. "How did you stop your Mirror?"

Daniel falls silent. An infectious silence that takes over the room. Andy doesn't mind. It gives him clarity to listen for the cats. No meows, no purring, only scratching sounds. He doesn't move or look, just listens and pin points the sound. It is coming from inside the walls. Andy looks at the couch again. The sounds, the feeling in his guts, all point to the obvious truth. The hairs are too short, too coarse to be cat hair.

"Eric… we need to go." Andy pulls on Eric's arm.

"My trial was not yours." Daniel sighs, "My trial was the Tem-ple. And I failed."

Eric remembers that icon from the key he saw Daniel holding in the photo. It matches the icon above the door Mastermind said Nico would have. The Temple is Nico's trial. "But you survived?"

"Eric." Andy pulls harder on Eric's arm as the scratching in the walls moves. Converges. Above them, the scratching and scurrying of lots of little claws turns to the stomping and grinding of larger feet.

"You survived?" Eric doesn't hear Andy or whatever is happening upstairs. He's fixed on Daniel's expression of distant, deep thoughts.

"When you don't survive, a Mirror is sent to replace you." Daniel says and nods to answer Eric's next question that he didn't even ask. "Yes, I'm a Mirror of Daniel Newman."

Stomps move across the floor upstairs and stop at the stairway behind Daniel. Darkness stretches downstairs as a massive body blocks the window at the top of the stairs. The shadow undulates and twists, turning Andy's stomach. He can't see the shadow's owner through the piles of clothes and trash lining the stairs. Upstairs is dark too. But something is there, waiting for them.

"Come on!" Andy tugs harder and stands, getting ready to run.

Eric, still oblivious to the heavy panting at the top of the stairs, stands with Andy. "You're not the real Daniel Newman?"

"Daniel failed the trial. He was captured in the Temple. I was sent to stop people from looking for him." Daniel says quietly and doesn't look at Eric as he pushes himself back into the recliner. "The trial cannot be started until the game is ready. Those are the rules." Daniel nods with certainty.

"Eric!" Andy steps in front of him and shakes him. "We have to go!" Eric finally wakes up to Andy. And now, he hears the stomping steps coming down the stairs, the panting hungry breath heaving from the thing eyeing them up. The creature fills the staircase as it comes down. It walks like a person, but its body is made of scurrying brown rats weaving in and out of each other.

"Rat blob!" Andy shouts and pulls Eric's arm towards the door. Eric finally wakes up to the situation and runs with Andy to the door. Daniel Newman watches them from his chair as if watching a mouse run from a cat.

The door is locked.

"Sorry boys, but my pet doesn't get to eat fresh meat too often." Daniel stands. His knees, neck, spine pop in a crackling crescendo. "And I can't let the secrets of this place to get out."

The Rat Blob stomps slowly towards Eric and Andy at the door. Each step taking significant effort as the blob coordinates the rats to move together.

"There!" Andy points to the kitchen window. Eric and Andy follow the path of soda cans and crumbling magazines to the kitchen. A splattering blob of rats is thrown at them, hitting the doorway and stretching into a living wall of rats. Red eyes stare at Andy and Eric from the wall of rats begging the boys to come closer, to touch them, to allow just a little bite.

Eric looks around the room and sees an old glass plate on the floor. Old peanut butter crust flakes from the brown glass plate as Eric picks it up. He looks at the wall of rats blocking the kitchen, then the Rat Blob slowly moving towards him. Daniel watches with curious delight.

Eric throws the plate through the wall of rats. It bursts open with rats tumbling away, dripping from the walls where they once clung.

"This way!" Eric says and rushes towards the kitchen window. He jumps through, making glass explode out into the overgrown garden. Andy follows him out and jumps, but a blob of rats covers the window just as Andy comes through. The rats catch his shoe and claw Andy back towards the window.

"Help!" Andy screams.

Eric jumps out of the grass and reaches for him, but the rats pull back. Eric sees they have his shoe and rips it off of Andy, letting the rats have the gnawed up Nike. Andy scrambles away and both boys run to the bike. Eric jumps on to drive as Andy jumps onto the back bars.

"GO!" Andy screams. Eric stomps down on the pedal and pumps his legs to get as much distance from that house as possible. He looks back to see if the Rat Blob follows and only sees Daniel Newman on his porch, laughing at them.

Eric doesn't see the cop car parked on the side of the road. They crash into it, sending him and Andy tumbling over the hood. Andy lands on Eric with a crushing smoosh.

But, before Eric sees the cop car he just fell over, he sees the cop standing over him and Andy.

"Shouldn't you boys be in school?" She says.

21

"Well?" The police officer folds her arms, cocks her head. She had black hair pulled back tight, dark brown skin and the standard tan and green uniform of the Junction Hollow Police Department. Giant sunglasses blocked out her eyes and the sun behind her blocked out the rest of her face.

If they could see her face, they knew she'd be scowling like adults do when they think they've caught you doing something wrong. The scowl that holds back the delighted smile reserved for when they get to punish a kid.

"I-I was just helping my friend with something." Eric looks up at the police officer, then at Andy, who's trying to untangle himself from Eric.

The police officer looks at them both and sighs. "Let me guess, you were acting a fool and ditching school?"

Eric shrugs, "Actually, I'm suspended." He smiles and looks for a way out. "But he's new, so I was just showing him around."

"Um, hmmm?" The police officer didn't believe them. "You two from Old Town?"

"That's right." Eric nods, hoping his lie will be convincing.

The officer looks at them again and shakes her head. "You know what I think? You were doing something more than just ditching school." She puts a hand on her hip and steps closer to the two boys. "You were doing something dangerous."

Eric and Andy see the intensity in her stance, her perfectly straight posture, signaling they are in serious trouble. They look at each other, their hearts beating fast as the officer takes a step closer to them. Andy considers making something up, but this is a cop. Lying is just going to make it worse.

"Yes ma'am. I was ditching school to hang out with my friend. He is suspended." Andy says, admitting defeat.

"Okay, so now I see which one of you is the smart one." She leans down to Andy. "Can I get your name?"

"Andy… uh Andrew Thompson."

The police officer smiles letting go of her intimidating facade. "Andy, it's good to meet you. I'm not going to arrest you or anything." She rests her hand on his arm to calm him. "But I do need to get you two home." She opens the back seat door of her cruiser. "Hop in. We'll go to the station, and I'll call your parents."

Andy climbs right in. Eric hesitates.

"Andy, can you encourage your friend to join you?" The tension in her voice switches to 'do what I say or else' mode. Eric doesn't need more encouraging after hearing her tone. He gets into the car. The police officer shut the door. "I'm Officer Dugan, by the way. Pleasure to meet you Andy and…" she trails off, looking at Eric.

"Eric."

Officer Dugan loads the bike into the car's trunk and then climbs into the driver's seat. She calls into dispatch with codes the boys don't understand. Andy looks to Eric with enormous eyes that say one thing… busted.

Andy takes comfort in talking to Officer Dugan on the ride. She's kind and enforces the value of school for the boys. She tells them about her own childhood, how she grew up in a dangerous place where school was the only place she could explore things like poetry, art, and mythology before she moved here to Junction Hollow. Eric perks up at that.

"What kinds of mythology did you study?" Eric asks.

Officer Dugan looks at him in the rear-view mirror. "I never was much for Greek mythology. Didn't really interest me. I really enjoyed learning about African mythology because, well, those were the myths of my history." She nods and smiles. "A lot of the history stuff in school was about Europe and America, but I wanted to learn about where my family came from. Mythology class was the only place we really talked about Africa."

Eric wonders if Officer Dugan grew up before Black History Month but considered his own classes. They didn't really talk about Africa much. Or Asia. Or South America. Or anywhere that wasn't western Europe and the United States. Eric nodded.

Andy lit up at Officer Dugan's story. "When you say African myths, does that include Egyptian myths?"

Officer Dugan shrugged and scrunched her nose. "I read a bit, but not really for me. Most of what I enjoyed were the folktales and stories in central Africa. Still read them sometimes."

Andy leans closer to her. "But do you know anything about the Eye of Horus or anything about trials?"

Officer Dugan thinks for a moment as they pull into the police station. The building looks nice, fresh white stones, gigantic windows to let light in. People walked around outside the police station, mostly drinking coffee, because nothing ever happened in Junction Hollow. The police were as bored as everyone else.

"Not the Eye of Horus, but trials put me in mind of the afterlife myth." Officer Dugan gets out of the car and opens their door. Eric and Andy climb out, looking eagerly at her to keep talking. She takes off her sunglasses, kind, smiling eyes, puts both boys at ease. As she walks them up to the police station steps, Eric notices how tall she is but not because she's really tall, just her posture is perfect and that makes her look like she stretches into the sky. "Let's go in." She motions them up the stairs.

"The myth is that when you die, your heart is weighed against the feather of Ma'at," she says, opening the door. "If your heart is heavier, you're eaten by Ammit and if it's lighter, you move on to the afterlife."

Eric gasps, "I've read about that!" Andy nods in excitement. Eric remembers the scale, the heart and feather on the metal door, his door. He thought the feather was the symbol of Ma'at, but now he's certain.

"It's just a story," Officer Dugan says, following the boys into the police station. She motions to a desk. "Have a seat and let's call your parents."

Eric sits down and sees a picture on Officer Dugan's desk. She's not in her uniform. Her black hair is loose and puffy around her head, just like the beautiful girl she's hugging. Eric's eyes go big as he nods towards the picture for Andy to see. Andy looks and *his* eyes go big, too.

"Is that your daughter?" Eric points to the picture.

Officer Dugan nods. "Stepdaughter. She's about your age.

You boys go to Junction Hollow Middle when you actually go to school?" She smiles.

"Yeah, but we're in different classes. I've seen her in the halls," Eric responds before Andy can fumble through an answer. Neither of them has been good at lying, but Eric hopes he's convincing in his half-truth. The girl in the picture is Anna.

"Oh," Officer Dugan sits down across from them, "You can talk to her about school. She's a good listener. Great kid. I bet you're good kids, too. Just made a mistake today."

She pushes a piece of paper to them and asks for their parent's name and number. Andy dutifully writes his down and hands the note to Eric. Eric takes it and thinks of who else he could write. But there isn't anyone else. Dad and Nico's all he's got. He writes his dad's information down.

Officer Dugan calls Andy's parents first. Eric can't pull his eyes away from Anna's picture. She's smiling. She's happy. She's not looking at him with anger and disgust for pushing Andy, for breaking his drone. This picture is the Anna Eric wishes he saw every day. Then the words come back to Eric, "step-mom?" He didn't know her dad got re-married. He'd never met her. Anna met Eric's dad. Anna met Andy's family too when Andy had that big picnic. But her parents have never been around after Anna's mom died. Andy's parents arrive at the police station first. His mom lectures him about school, how it is the key to Andy's future, and Eric laughs. *Andy's so focused on school and college that it's all he does.* Even Andy's hobbies are about getting into a good college. Andy just smiles and looks back at Eric. He puts his fingers up in the universal 'call me' sign. Andy's not done with adventuring yet.

Eric's dad arrives soon after.

"Thank you, Officer." Eric's dad says.

Officer Dugan nods. "He's a good kid, Mr. Clark. Don't go too hard on him." She pats Eric's shoulder. "I'm sure he's learned an important lesson." Officer Dugan looks at Eric. Her smile fades. "When you're trying to be sneaky, make sure you watch where you're going."

Eric nods. "Thanks Officer Dugan. For the stories and for helping Andy and I get home."

Mort Clark smiles politely but grinds his teeth behind the smile, "Thank you again. Eric, let's get home."
Eric climbs into the car and braces for screaming or lecturing, but just like with his suspension, it doesn't come. Instead, his dad climbs into the car, starts it, and drives home.

Quick, shallow breaths choke back the tears filling his dad's eyes. "I'm sorry, dad," Eric whispers.

"I don't understand, Eric," his dad says, "is this a rebellion thing? You've never snuck out before. Never been in trouble outside of fighting bullies." He shakes his head. "I just don't understand."

"Dad, it's not a rebellion thing. I swear." Eric looks at his dad, really looks at him, and sees the pain in his dad's eyes. The wrinkles that have appeared since mom left. The gray strands growing in his pale blonde hair. He sees his dad for the first time in a long time.

"And then there's the back talk." Eric's dad says. Eric freezes at that. He didn't think he was back talking… "This morning. What you said about your mom? That's just not you!"

Eric wants to scream that *wasn't* him. That was his Mirror ruining his life. But Dad wouldn't understand that. Eric knew his dad was a practical type. A software developer who earns a living through the power of logic and reason. Talking about monsters, magic, and talking about gems isn't something Eric's dad would do. So, Eric says nothing. He looks out the window at the houses passing by, listening to the rhythmic whooshing of the FOR SALE signs planted in every yard.

"When we get home, I want you in your room and stay there. I haven't been checking in on you because I thought you were trustworthy. I see I was wrong." His dad says as he drags his hand over his face, wiping away tears and exhaustion. "No more hanging out with Nico, no TV, no internet. Give me your phone when you get in."

Eric nods. Cut off. Locked down. And worse, what happens when his Mirror gets home from whatever it's doing today?

When they pull into their driveway, Eric follows his dad into the house. Mirror Nico is on the couch, eating more potato chips. Eric wonders where he got the fresh bag.

"Uh oh." Mirror Nico says and laughs, "Busted."

Eric scrunches his face at his fake brother and walks back to his room. He reaches into his pocket to pull out his phone and remembers it's still in Mastermind's cave. He shakes his head and walks to his room. Before he can shut the door, shock knocks Eric back. He gapes at the drawings and rude sayings on the walls. Black marker smeared and scribbled everywhere. His dad walks up behind him and gasps.

"Are you kidding me Eric!?" Dad yells, "I can't even deal with this right now! Stay in here!" He stabs his finger at Eric's room.

The oppressing black marker screams at him from everywhere.

Eric's a loser

Eric failed

It's all your fault, Eric

Many use profanity and swear words. His dad walks out and slams the door, but Eric can hear him breathing heavily on the other side. Outside his door, Eric hears a lock turn. "You need to reflect on what you want in life, Eric. This isn't who I raised you to be."

Eric nods. "No. It's not." He flops on his bed. "Now what...?"

But Eric didn't know. He felt no closer to solving this trial now than he did when he started two days ago.

"Pssst. Hey." Mirror Nico calls from the other side of the door. "Don't forget the time limit." Mirror Nico giggles.

Eric sits bolt upright. "What time limit? There's no time limit?" *More rules I don't know about?*

"Time limit. You have three days to complete the trial. That's one of the rules." Mirror Nico explains through his laughing.

"Mastermind didn't say anything about a time limit." Eric dismisses him.

"And Mastermind told you all the rules? He only has to share four. Any more has to be requested by the player. That's you. That's one of the fun things about the trial is you don't know all the rules." Mirror Nico says. "Duh! It's been that way, like forever." Mirror Nico scoffs and laughs, "Games are more fun when you play against people who don't know the rules."

More fun for who? Eric scoffs. *It's designed to be lost.* Eric sits back in confusion. He knows he's going to have to find a way through this trial before his Mirror takes over completely. And now, if Mirror Nico is right, he has less than one day to do it.

As the clock ticks faster, Eric lays back down and wonders, *what do I do now?*

22

"Why'd I ever think I could do this?" Eric rolls over on his bed. Back on the mountain, Mirror Nico told him there was no point in trying. He was right. The real Nico had too much faith in Eric and that faith will be rewarded with being trapped in Mastermind's cavern.

Eric looks in the mirror. He's a mess. Dark circles line his eyes, and his hair is so dirty it stands up on its own. "Screw it." Eric says to himself. He's not going to give up without trying everything. *The real Nico wouldn't give up on me, and I can't give up on him.*

Going to his desk, Eric gets a pencil and paper to jot down what he knows so far. He writes the rules; he writes what he found out in the library about the cycles of missing people. He writes what he remembers of the conversation with Daniel Newman and the trials. And he looks at the facts all laid out together.

None of this makes sense.

He takes a deep breath and keeps looking, but nothing ties it together. Nothing fits to explain what's going on or what to do next.

What do the missing people have to do with the trial? Who is RM from the book? How could fresh notes show up in a book in his handwriting when he didn't write it?

"I should have stayed. Nico could have figured this all out." Eric looks at the paper, then rips it up. *Does Nico feel abandoned? Of course he does, because I left him behind.* He was abandoned by all the people who've left. Not just by Mom. But, by Eric. Nico was counting on Eric coming back, like Eric was counting on his mom coming back. Now, Eric's not sure either is ever going to happen.

Knock, Knock

Eric jumps. He walks to the door and puts his hand on the knob, but doesn't turn it. "Who is it?"

"Mastermind." A voice comes from the other side. Then laughing. His laughing. It's Mirror Eric. "I'm kidding stupid. It's me. Hey, I found out where Anna lives. I'm still sore where she sucker punched me. Going to repay the favor. Wanted to let you know some pain's heading your way," Mirror Eric cackles. "But don't worry, she'll hurt more."

Eric growls. "Leave her alone!" But the laughs fade as Mirror Eric walks away. The front door slams and Eric hears his dad ask Mirror Nico what that was. Sleepily, Mirror Nico says it was the wind.

Eric shakes his head. Anna needs him, Nico needs him, and he's not sure what to do next. He thinks about Nico, alone in the cavern, waiting for Eric to save him. Anna's all by herself. He looks to his window and unlocks it. Eric never ran away before, never even thought of it, but if he doesn't go, he'll never save Nico. He'll never save Anna.

He doesn't want to leave dad alone. But he has to go. He has to do what's right.

Is that what Mom thought? Did she leave to do what's best for everyone or just for herself? Does she know he and Nico want her to come back? No matter how long she's been gone, they want her to come back.

Opening the window, Eric puts one leg out as there's a gentle knocking at his door.

"Eric?" His dad says, "I'm going to order takeout. You in the mood for pizza?"

"Pizza sounds good," Eric says. Guilt swells in him, making it hard to swallow. "Thanks dad."

"I also," Dad pauses, "…we need to talk about what's going on with you."

Eric sags under the weight of his own disappointment. *Dad wants to help me and I'm running away.* "Okay." Eric says slowly.

"I'm worried about you." His dad says, and Eric feels the concern, feels his dad's love in those words. "When the pizza gets here, I'll bring it in, and we can chat."

"I'd like that," Eric says as he shakes his head and looks to the sky to hold the tears in his eyes. "Love you, Dad." And Eric slips out into the night, landing in a stumble, falling flat on his face. As he looks up, he sees someone standing over him. Someone holding a sword.

23

The sword glints in the bloody orange of a late afternoon sun.

"Which one?" Andy demands.

Eric looks up, seeing the slight frame of his friend. "It's the real Eric." Eric whispers.

"Then why didn't you answer when I called you?" Andy points the sword at Eric. Poking it towards him. "The bully version of you answered." Andy scoffs. "And he was a jerk."

"I lost my phone on Mirror Mountain. I've been in my room all afternoon." Eric motions between Andy and himself, "Look, I'm me. We got caught by Anna's stepmom earlier today."

Andy nods. Lowers his sword. Eric stands and moves away from his window, keeping his eyes on Andy's sword. "Where'd you get a sword?"

"Oh, it's not real." Andy swings it around. "Part of my cosplay wardrobe." Andy follows Eric up the street.

"Did you sneak out?" Eric asks.

Andy nods. "Yes." Excitement bubbling out of him. "Operation Prison Break! The thrilling adventures of a bad boy. That's the new Andy!"

Eric grimaces, wondering if he's made a monster.

"And I brought some other stuff, too." Andy shrugs his backpack off his back and opens it up. "All the essentials."

Eric spots a telescope, rope, rope cutters, canteens, and other survival things. He grins. "Nice."

Andy smiles with pride at this praise. "Now we're ready for adventure. Just need to find your Mirror and lead him back to the mountain." Andy looks around as they hide in the bushes.

Headlights pull up to Eric's house. The pizza guy gets out and delivers the pizzas. Next, Eric's dad will go to his room and find it empty. He'll be disappointed. Angry. But Eric must do what's right.

"Come on." Eric nods up the street, away from his dad. "We've got to get to Anna's."

"Anna's?" Andy looks confused. "Why?"

"That's where my Mirror is going. He said he was going to get her back for what she did. But that's not going to happen." Eric says as they walk faster.

Andy swirls his fake sword around in a figure eight as he runs. "Let's go save the maiden!" He points the sword forward and Eric follows in a run.

"Got any other weapons?" Eric asks. Andy shakes his head, but stops suddenly mid shake.

"Well… maybe?" Andy says as they run towards Anna's house. A devious smile creeps over Andy's lips, and Eric again wonders what he's unleashed.

24

"What are you going to do?" Eric asks as they slow down to a walk. They see Officer Dugan's all too familiar car sitting in Anna's driveway. Eric gulps with a loud click in his throat.

"I brought my water gun." Andy pats his backpack. "It's loaded with hot sauce."

Eric groans. "That's going to burn." Sure, the Mirror will suffer as Andy sprays hot sauce in his eyes, but Eric braces knowing the Mirror won't be the only one to feel the burn. "Just a reminder. Anything we do to him happens to me. So, let's be careful."

Andy frowns. "Yeah… I forgot about that."

Just as they pass the driveway, they see Mirror Eric picking up rocks in Anna's yard. Eric knows those rocks are heading straight for her window. He doesn't wait, launching himself into action. He doesn't hear Andy call for him to come back, he just feels the crushing impact to his own gut as he tackles Mirror Eric spearing him through the stomach.

They fall to the ground in a heap, rolling around, each trying to gain control over the other. Eric is fighting his Mirror, but he can feel it too. The hatred and anger that bubbles beneath the surface of Mirror Eric.

Andy rushes up, aiming his hot sauce water gun. He stops and pumps a stream of Texas Tom's Forty Alarm Fire Sauce right into Mirror Eric's snarling mouth. Eric chokes and gasps rolling off his Mirror and scraping his tongue as Mirror Eric howls in burning torment.

Anna's window opens. "What's going on out there!?" she yells and sees Andy. He stands upright and waves to her.

"Hi Anna." Andy points to the two Erics, "We need to talk." Andy smiles. "It's kind of weird." He squints one eye, thinking about how to describe what's going on.

Anna's eyes go wide seeing the writhing Erics on the ground. One near Andy's feet. One rolling away trying to get to the water hose.

"Eric, let me know when you're ready." Andy lowers the water gun to Mirror Eric and whispers. "So, you feeling lucky? Well, do ya?"

The water hose squeaks on, dribbling fat splats on the ground. "Go!" Eric shouts as he lifts the hose over his mouth and gulps the cool waterfall.

Andy unleashes another burst, gagging Mirror Eric. The other Eric growls in pain and chugs from the water hose as fast as it comes out. He spits and guzzles.

"What…?" Anna's confusion looks like it is physically painful to observe the chaos. Mirror Eric punches Andy's knee. Andy shouts in pain and falls as Mirror Eric scrambles up and runs into the trees behind Anna's house.

"What's going on out there?" Officer Dugan appears beside

Anna with a well-used baseball bat. Eric would run if he didn't need a constant stream of water to drown the fire in his throat.

"Hi, Officer Dugan," Andy calls up as he rolls on the ground, holding his knee.

"You know these boys?" Dugan asks Anna. Anna rolls her eyes, sighs, and nods.

***

A few minutes later, Eric and Andy are sitting on Anna's couch. Anna stands with her stepmom, both of them in the same arms crossed, head cocked, legs apart stance that makes Eric more nervous than he was in the police car earlier.

"Who's starting?" Dugan asks. Her gaze juts between the two. "The smart one or," she suppresses a laugh, "the wet one?"

"Why were there two of you?" Anna's voice is just as sharp as her stepmom's. Eric sits up straighter. "And why are you with this guy after the other day?" Anna looks at Andy.

Andy opens his mouth to answer.

"What happened the other day?" Dugan cuts him off. Andy starts to answer.

"This guy," Anna throws her hands at Eric, "who I thought was a good guy, was pushing him around." Eric raises his hand and opens his mouth.

"Wait? Is this that boy you were talking about last night?" Dugan asks Anna, but neither of them has taken their eyes off Andy or Eric. They're talking to each other but never losing sight of their prey. Anna nods. "Oh sweetie, he's not worth your tears."

Eric tries to talk again.

"I see that now," Anna snarls. "I guess he put on a good show."

Andy pipes in, "Hi, can I say something?"

Anna and Dugan shout, "No!"

The four sit in quiet for a few moments. A clock ticks away the seconds of silence. Andy shuffles looking down to the coffee table between the couch where Andy and Eric sat and the open area where Anna and Dugan stood glaring at them.

"You explain Eric. Why were there two of you?" Anna leans towards him, and Eric leans back, remembering the punch. It wasn't meant for him, but he still can feel it on his tender jaw.

Eric waits another moment to make sure he can talk. "The other me isn't me. It's a doppelgänger from Mirror Mountain. Actually, it's called a Flipman because—"

"What?" Anna interrupts.

"Yeah, there's more…" Andy nods with a slight grin.

Eric tells her and Dugan about the trial of Mirror Mountain. He tells her about Mastermind and everything he's learned so far. Dugan sits as he tells his story. Her angry expression melting to rapt interest. But Anna doesn't move. Her anger burrows deeper. She wonders if this is some elaborate prank. Something Eric's doing because she's leaving.

As the sun sets, Anna and Dugan look at each other to see if they believe Eric and Andy. Dugan nods. Anna looks confused.

"You believe this?" Anna says to Dugan.

"The story sounds crazy, but it makes sense." Dugan says.

Eric perks up at that. *Does it make sense?*

"If I were investigating this, I'd be looking for a timeline, motivation, and alibis. If what Eric here says is true about the Mirror being his opposite and you've told me before, how he stands up to bullies, it makes sense that his opposite would be a bully. You said he was suspended standing up for this one, and here we are again. He's standing up for this one and you." Dugan leans back in her chair. "What I said earlier was right. You're a good kid, Eric."

Eric smiles, but it doesn't stay as his eyes go to Anna. "I swear Anna. This is all the truth."

"Yeah." Andy chimes in. "Totally true." He pulls out his water gun. "Especially the part where I let that Mirror have it with my hot sauce." Andy winks at Dugan and she chuckles.

"So, what now?" Anna asks.

Eric shrugs. "Yeah, that's the problem we keep having. And I've got to figure something out to help Nico before tomorrow." Eric's head drops into his hands.

"Easy." Dugan says. "We drag your Mirror's butt to the mountain and throw him through that wall or whatever."

"Wall of Twins." Andy corrects, then waves an apology under Dugan's glare. "And I might have something that can help there." Andy fishes in his bag.

"This is crazy," Anna sighs and plops into a chair beside her stepmom. "I can't believe you're going for this." Anna looks at Eric. "I'm not buying it. A cursed mountain isn't what makes people do mean things. That's just people being people, and everyone's got a dark side in them, Eric. Even you."

Dugan sighs and reaches for Anna's hand. Anna snaps it away.

"I'll go along for now, but this is it, Eric. After tonight, I'm done with all this. I don't want any more crazy. I've got enough of my own to deal with," Anna says.

Eric nods. His heart sinks. He doesn't want things to end like this between them, but at least he gets one more night to set things right. Maybe one more night is all he needs, but it doesn't matter if that's what he needs. One more night is all he has.

25

Together, the four hatch a plan. Anna was the least interested. She still didn't trust Eric's story and didn't understand why Andy was sticking up for him. But Andy and Dugan were more than happy to help. Their enthusiasm makes up for Anna's lack thereof.

The plan begins with Eric finding Mirror Eric, and he has to do this alone. At first, he protests the solo mission, citing his recent track record for doing things by himself. It's not good. He knows anything he does by himself would fail because everything has. *Why does everyone have so much faith in me? I don't deserve it. Definitely didn't earn it.*

But none the less, Eric is alone, going to where his Mirror is hiding. He knew where he'd go to lick his wounds and where he'd go to get a long drink to drown that searing feeling: home. Even jerks like his evil twin needed help, and Mirror Nico would be the only person to help him.

And Eric was right. There was Mirror Eric in his bedroom, eating the pizza that Dad left for the real Eric when he walked in and saw that Eric had run away. Mirror Eric was admiring his marker work when a rock hit him in the head. Eric felt this too.

Mirror Eric snaps around and glowers at Eric.

"Let's go Flipman." Eric throws the next rock at Mirror Eric's face. He missed. Eric is thankful for that. Mirror Eric climbs out the window and snorts in anger.

"When I hit you, I don't feel a thing." Mirror Eric smiles. He punches his hand, making a dull clapping noise as the stars pop through twilight.

"Yep." Eric remembers how clear rule number four was. *Whatever is done to the Mirror returns to him. Why does that rule exist? Why do any of them exist? Why do the trials exist?*

Mirror Eric runs to him, smiling, relishing the beating he's about to give Eric. Eric runs as planned and trips over the neighbor kid's power wheel bike. That wasn't part of the plan. Mirror Eric busts up laughing but doesn't slow down. Eric claws back to his feet and takes off running, checking to make sure that his Mirror is still chasing.

"Who's running now?" Mirror Eric barks out. "You running from me now? And I thought you were all about fighting?"

Eric turns the corner of the block and nods to Andy, who's in the bushes. Andy nods to Anna across the street. Eric stops and puts his hands up, ready to fight. "Come on!" Eric shouts to his Mirror, who runs faster to land a crushing punch to his face. "Come on!"

As Mirror Eric gets within a few feet, Eric nods, triggering Andy and Anna to snap up Andy's rope, catching Mirror Eric across the gut. Eric's breath is squeezed out of him as he feels the rope snap on his own stomach. Both Erics crumble to the ground.

"Hurry!" Andy shouts to Anna. She rushes over and zip ties Mirror Eric's wrists and ankles. Stepping back away, she gasps at the exact copy of Eric's face. How he moves, how he wheezes for breath, all exactly the same.

"Crazy…" Anna gasps.

"Yeah, I know," Andy says and comes to her. "I couldn't believe it at first either, but yeah, that's not Eric." Mirror Eric struggles against the restraints. Anna made them tight, and they cut into Mirror Eric's skin. She smiles and thinks how he deserves this. Eric comes over and she sees his wrists are bleeding where the restraints would be.

"Where's your mom?" Eric says as he shakes his wrists. Anna points to the little sedan her stepmom drives when she's not in the cruiser. The lights flick on, and it silently rolls up to them. Electric cars are great for stealth. Anna, Andy, and Eric load Mirror Eric into the hatchback, then climb into the tiny car.

"Sorry, usually just me and Anna," Dugan says.

"Better than our last ride together," Andy chuckles and Dugan laughs.

"Smart and funny." Dugan smiles at Anna, who sits beside her. "You sure you picked the right one?"

Anna blushes. "Mom."

Eric blushes too, but Andy just laughs in pure joy. This adventure, Operation Mirror Crusher, is going exactly as planned. He hopes it stays that way.

***

The team drives out of town and up Mirror Mountain. Eric tries to remember the trail he and Nico took, but everything looks different at night. If he had his phone, he could have used the GPS to find where Nico had parked. But he just goes on instinct and gets lucky when they pull up behind Nico's beat up blue hatchback. It's still where Eric and Nico left in almost three nights ago.

They open the hatch to see Mirror Eric calmly lying there like he just woke up from a pleasant nap. "Kidnapping isn't very nice." He sneers to the four. "And you, you should know better." He looks at Eric. "No one can complete the trial for you. Rule number three." He laughs.

"I know. We're going on alone." Eric pulls him out of the car and cuts his foot restraints, then his hand restraints with a knife. He hands the knife back to Dugan. "Remember, when I come back, we'll go back to my house and explain everything to my dad. I'll meet you back here, but I'll be alone."

Mirror Eric suppresses a smile as his own plan comes together. Andy fishes in his backpack for something, he hands it to Eric who shoves it in his pocket too fast for Mirror Eric to see what it is. Dugan pulls out a stepladder from the car, which makes Mirror Eric laugh, wondering if this car was not only hybrid electric but also part clown car. He's brought out of the amusing thought when Eric pushes him into the woods.

As the Erics fade into the woods, Anna calls out, "Good luck Eric. Be careful."

"See you soon," Eric calls back.

"Yeah, I'll see you real soon." Mirror Eric cackles.

26

Neither of them talk as they follow Nico and Eric's original trail. They can hear mumbles and whispers behind them as Dugan, Andy, and Anna wait for their return. The sound of woodpeckers hammering at the trees behind them echoes in the night. Mirror Eric stops walking and thinks it is too late for a woodpecker. Eric's hand smacks him in the back.

"Keep walking." Eric says.

Mirror Eric does, and the noises behind them fade as the darkness of Mirror Mountain swallows them. They get to the Wall of Twins and Mirror Eric stops. He turns to Eric and grins. "Now what?"

"Now you go in." Eric points beyond the Wall of Twins.

"But, aren't those Twins magical?" Mirror Eric laughs. "Rule number two." He points to the figures dangling in the wind.

Eric pauses. Mirror Eric knows he's thinking, knows the real Eric never considered this. How could his feeble mind not put two and two together? The game is designed to be lost. The player never has a chance. That's why Mastermind never tells all the rules. That's why the Mirror always gets a head start. The player never wins. Only the mountain wins. Only Gamemaster wins.

"You are as stupid as I thought." Mirror Eric walks up to Eric, who stands, his mouth gaping. As Mirror Eric gets closer, Eric's jaw clenches. Mirror Eric punches him with everything he's got. He catches Eric by surprise and knocks him out cold. Eric crumbles to the ground, KO'd by Mirror Eric. "Don't worry Eric. I'll ruin your life and everyone else's. I won't leave anyone out." Mirror Eric hops over Eric and laughs. A wolf howls further up the mountain. "Oh, and it looks like your friends will get just one of us back after all." Mirror Eric laughs hysterically, a hyena laugh as he sprints back to the car.

Jumping over fallen trees, catching a branch or two in the face, feeling the slashing as he runs through the woods. From far away, he hears Andy say, "All done." The sound of a ladder collapsing can be heard. Mirror Eric sees the car headlights come on, a beacon to his escape. Once they leave, once he gets in that car and they drive away, Eric won't be able to change anything. Time will be up. The third night will have passed, and Eric will be stuck in the White Void, and his brother will be imprisoned on Mirror Mountain forever.

"Eric!" Anna calls and cheers. "Did you do it?"

"Yeah! Let's go! Gotta get out of here fast! Something's coming!" Mirror Eric shouts in his best imitation of the real Eric.

"Come on!" Andy shouts, waving him to the open car door. Dugan is in the driver's seat, ready.

Mirror Eric gets to the last line of trees, sprinting full speed when he sees Andy smiling. *He's smiling?* Not a happy smile… a mischievous smile. Andy's hiding something behind his leg. Mirror Eric recognizes it. It's a hammer. *The woodpecker? What was he hammering? Something's wrong.* Mirror Eric tries to stop, but he's going too fast and the ground is too muddy. He slides forward, glancing up to something glittering in the moonlight, it's a string of something above him. *That's what they were doing. Hanging something in the trees.* Mirror Eric struggles to stop, but the mud and momentum keeps him moving forward. He skids through the last row of trees before the car. A white flash burst in his eyes and suddenly he's in Mastermind's cavern.

Eric and Nico stand in the cave, smiling. They're holding in a laugh, infuriating Mirror Eric more. Mastermind floats between the stalactite and stalagmite with a soft, pulsing, pink glow.

"Cheat!" Mirror Eric screamed!

27

Eric fishes in his pocket and pulls out what Andy gave him. He holds it up for Mastermind to see. The pink glow of the gem shows a 3D printed stick figure, like on the strings of the Wall of Twins.

"Mastermind said you needed to cross '*A*' Wall of Twins. There are many on the mountain, but what's important is that it was a literal wall of twins." Eric twirls the 3D printed figure and tosses it to Mirror Eric. "Andy printed them. Then while you and I were walking, my friends hung the wall, but you walked through it without any help from them. No one performed the trial but me. I tricked you into leaving me in the woods and running back to the car."

"But, the other Wall—" Mirror Eric says, grasping to catch up with what's happened.
"Andy and Dugan figured that out. They said it was magical, and that'd violate rule two. So, we made a non-magical version of the wall. Last I checked, 3D printed plastic isn't magic." Eric says and glances at Nico.
"No, it is not." Nico says, nodding in approval.
Mastermind pulses a slow glow as it thinks about the claim.

Eric continued, "When you punched me, I embellished your weak punch and then when you ran off, I rolled into the Wall of Twins to meet you here. I just used my head while you used your fists." Eric held out his hand for a celebratory high five. Nico smacked it with an echoing crack that made both brothers laugh.

"Is this what happened?" Mastermind asks Mirror Eric.

Mirror Eric looks for a loophole, looks for a failing, but in the end, only finds his own. He was so eager to win that he didn't think beyond a game between Eric and himself. The friends were helping, but ultimately, Eric was the one who orchestrated his downfall.

"Yes," Mirror Eric says, defeated, as he evaporates in wisps of steam.

"Then it is done." Mastermind glows blinding bright. Nico and Eric cover their eyes as a giant key fizzles into reality in front of the pink gem. "The keys are released as declared by the rules. The Trial of Ma'at has been completed." In a bright light, the key snaps apart into five sections. Eric can see how they fit together even as they drift apart.

Four of the keys fizzle back out of reality. One flies to Nico's hand. The end of the key looks like an old Greek temple, but as Eric looks closer, he notices the hieroglyphs, the cartouche, it's an Egyptian temple. Nico takes his key to the door that erupted from the ground when Nico and Eric returned to Mastermind's cave.

"Nico Clark. Your trial begins when you unlock that door. Your Mirror will be retracted until then." Mastermind says.

"No!" Eric shouts. "Leave his Mirror. Please." Eric looks at Nico with a sly smile. "For our dad's sake. Let's have some normalcy."

"So be it." Mastermind says.

"Be careful," Eric says. "I love you, bro!" The cave starts to fade out as Nico walks towards his door. "Ask about the rules!" Eric feels the world around him go dark as the cave vanishes. In the darkness, someone is screaming. A high-pitched howling scream.

Eric moves quickly, pushing away but running into a car door. He's in the backseat of a car. The high-pitched scream is coming from Andy.

"Aaahhhh!! Aaaaahhh!!! Is it you?" Andy howls.

Eric smiles. Pulls him in for a hug. "It's me! It worked!" Dugan and Anna are in the front seat and turn around to see him. "It worked!"

28

On the ride home, Eric explains everything. The keys, Nico's trial, the Egyptian symbols.

Dugan perks up at that. "Maybe I should bone up," she says.

They drive straight to Eric's house where Dugan, Anna, Andy, and Eric all explain things to Eric's dad. Eric leads the conversation with supporting statements from Andy, Dugan, and Anna as needed. There is no mention of Mirror Nico.

Eric's dad doesn't believe all this at first, giving Dugan strange glances to confirm the story as it unravels. He asks how everyone got involved, asks why they didn't come to him sooner. As the story continues, the disbelief starts to fall away as everyone contributes their part of the story. A story, so bizarre and out there, that Eric's dad stops questioning if it is real and starts questioning what would happen next.

By the end, Eric's dad pulls him in for a hug. "I'm sorry Eric." he says, "I should have asked what was going on sooner and just been there for you."

Eric shakes his head. "No. I should have told you sooner. I just, with everyone leaving, I forgot the good things here."

Eric's dad offers everyone drinks and the rest of the pizza from earlier. Dugan and Anna leave soon after the story while Andy hangs around for a few slices of pizza and to tell the story of how he used the hot sauce gun to stop Mirror Eric. *That story will get a lot of retellings*, Eric laughs.

After the third telling of what is now known as Operation Hot Sauce, Eric's dad drives Andy home with a few to-go slices of pizza.

"See you tomorrow?" Andy says to Eric.

"Totally," Eric says, "Thanks Andy!"

Andy nods with a salute and a wink. Eric laughs and looks forward to hearing the hot sauce gun story again tomorrow. The smile fades as a sinking feeling settles over Eric. *I won't hear the story again tomorrow.* He waves goodbye to Andy as his dad pulls away. Standing on the porch, watching Andy and his dad, Eric tries to etch Andy's face in his mind, memorizing his clumpy black curls, his thick black rim glasses and his always too excited smile. *Andy's leaving too, but sooner than anyone thinks.* In his heart, Eric knows this is the last time he'll ever see Andy.

How do I know that? Eric wonders as he looks up at Mirror Mountain. A few streets down, a man with a scraggly black beard is standing under a streetlight. He's watching Eric from glittering eyes deep in the shadows of his hoodie. Eric stares back. The man turns, slowly pushing off the streetlight and walks off. *Just someone out for a walk.* He tells himself and looks back at Mirror Mountain, wondering how Nico is doing.

Am I done with you? Eric asks the mountain. *I think we're just getting started.*

***

Back home, Eric's dad cleans up from the company. Eric goes to his room to scrub the walls.

"So gross." Eric gets a sponge and a bucket of soapy water. When he comes back to his room, Mirror Nico is sitting on Eric's bed.

"Nothing about me?" Mirror Nico smiles.

Eric turns to him, a wicked smile overtaking Eric's face. A smile that Mirror Nico doesn't like. "Oh, no. I have different plans for you." Eric walks up to Mirror Nico. "You're going to tell me about the rules, about Mastermind, about Gamemaster…" Eric's smile grows, pushing the corners of his lips almost to his eyes. "And you're going to tell me everything about the Temple."

Mirror Nico backs away from Eric. "Or… or what? You going to hurt me?"

Eric shrugs. "No. I don't want to hurt Nico, but I'm betting there are other things that can motivate you." Eric steps out of his room, returning a moment later with a fresh bag of potato chips. He shakes it at Mirror Nico.

Mirror Nico's mouth waters and he grabs for it, but Eric snaps it back.

"You're a Flipman, which means you're the opposite of my brother. Nico's loyal, positive, brave… I bet you're none of that." Eric pushes the chips towards him. "Like, I bet you'll tell me what I want for a lifetime supply of chips."

"What do you want to know?" Mirror Nico takes the chips. Eric sits down on the bed as chip crumbs rain down over his blanket. Eric shivers at the idea of sleeping in those crumbs tonight.

"Let's start with the rules." Eric says.

EPILOGUE

Anna and Dugan get home late. The talk with Mort and Eric was longer than Dugan expected. Maybe she was more prepared to believe in magic than other people. Maybe it was the family legends or that weird psychic reading she got on summer vacation all those years ago, but the existence of magic makes sense to her. The existence of monsters even more so.

As Dugan opens the front door, she notices a bright light coming from the kitchen. Did she leave the kitchen light on when they left earlier? Anna goes upstairs, wiped out from the night and understandably so. Dugan collapses on the couch, ready to crash out from the long, strange day.

"Don't forget to take a shower." Dugan calls up to Anna. "It will help you relax." She reaches for the TV remote but it's out of reach. She waves it away and flops back on the couch, letting her arm fall over her face.

"Okay mom," Anna calls down.

Dugan feels the warmth in those words. Not thanks stepmom, or thanks Dugan, or thanks Naomi—thanks mom. She lucked out in the stepdaughter category and knows it.

Anna comes back down the stairs with the energetic hop that always follows her. "Forgot something down here."

Dugan waves but is too exhausted to lift her arm. It just flaps weakly as sleep starts to settle over her.

"Hey mom…" Anna's voice quivers.

All of Dugan's strength floods back through her body as she springs from the couch and jumps over the chair to reach Anna in the kitchen.

A golden key floating above the counter stops Dugan at the edge of the kitchen. She stands with Anna both gaping at the glowing key spinning above some dirty pans. Getting closer, Dugan and Anna see the key's handle is a triangle with a square on the base. Inside, the shape is a carved-out shape that looks like rough stalactites. Magical golden dust floats around the key like the sands of an hourglass.

"Is that one of Eric's keys?" Anna asks.

Dugan nods. Anna reaches for the key.

Dugan grabs her arm. "Together," Dugan says.

They touch it together. Bright white light pulses throughout the kitchen as the room quakes and the refrigerator transforms into a wooden door with iron banding. Above the door is the same icon as the key.

"What do you think?" Anna glances to Dugan, then back to the key. "Is this, should we call someone?"

Dugan shakes her head. "I don't think this is something we say no to." She shrugs. "Besides, I'm up for some adventure. You?"

Anna steps to the door and presses the key into the triangle shaped hole. The door opens to white light and the two walk in.

AI & YOU: PROMPT ENGINEERING

Hi! Tim here. I wrote this book with the help of Artificial Intelligence (AI). As a storyteller, I am always curious about tools and techniques to improve how I connect with my audience. I saw AI as another brain to help me think through and challenge my ideas.

But, like any tool, you need to know how to use AI for storytelling to make it work effectively. If you didn't know how to use a pencil, you probably wouldn't be able to draw with it very well. If you didn't know how to use a potter's wheel, don't expect amazing pottery. AI is the same and, like a pencil, like a potter's wheel, the key tool to understand when working with AI for Creativity is Prompt Engineering.

Before we get started, a note of warning. You are accountable for whatever YOU create with AI. As a human, you are responsible for your use of technology and the amazing abilities AI gives you. You cannot blame the machine for what it made and YOU are accountable for how YOU use this tool. Use these tools responsibly and for the good of all.

What is Prompt Engineering?

The words Prompt Engineering are a fancy way to say "ask the AI to do some action". Your prompt could be:

> *Write a story about a pirate and a ninja fighting over treasure in a floating city.*

Or perhaps you're asking the AI to draw something for you:

> *Draw an oil painting of a woman fixing a fire engineer with a puppy watching her.*

Like all communication, you need to be clear to your audience. When working with AI, you need to be clear with the AI system. This means to ask for what you mean and be clear without ambiguity. Requesting a "hotdog" is a lot different for AI than a "hot dog".

How to build a prompt

Start with the most important things first. What is the main thing you want to occur. With our first example above, we wanted to write a story and so that was the first thing in the prompt. If we started with talking about pirates and ninja's, we aren't saying how we want that content formatted. Let's try a few mutations of our prompt:

> *Write a song about a pirate and a ninja fighting over treasure in a cloud city.*

How about...

Write a haiku about a pirate and a ninja
fighting over treasure in a cloud city

These outputs will be very different from our original story. Remember, start with the most important thing first.

Next, move on to the subject you want to focus on. In the prompt, we want a story (that's the first thing we ask for) but then; we are getting more specific. We don't want just any story. We want a story about *a pirate and a ninja fighting over treasure.*

We could ask for anything here. Let's explore a few mutations of this prompt:

Write a story about a pirate and a ninja team-
ing up to win a treasure

Or, how about we transform even further:

Write a story about a pirate and a ninja creat-
ing a treasure

This content is important because we want to be clear about what we're asking the AI to produce. You can be as specific as you want:

Write a story about a pirate named Jon who is
tall with blue hair and a ninja named Lucy who
is short and a magical elf

When writing a prompt, I try to start as bare bones as possible. This helps the AI provide me with some creative ideas that maybe weren't in my head to start. I layer in more content to help refine what the AI produces.

Don't forget, AI helps you, it doesn't replace you. If you already know the pirate's name is Jon, tell the AI. You don't have to do what the machine says! This is your story. The AI is just helping you. Give it whatever information you want to give it to shape YOUR story. I start barebones, but perhaps you have a clear vision of your story. It is okay to be more directive with AI.

You have the first part of the prompt to ask for what you want, then the second part provides specifics, not layer in more context to be even more specific. For our example, we see that the pirate and ninja are fighting for treasure in a cloud city. The cloud city is more information for the prompt to flesh out our story.

Use this extra context to help flesh out your ideas. I often leave this off when I start to allow the ideas to come.

Let's look at a different example to see how these parts map to a totally different prompt:

> *Rewrite the following in 3rd person from Jon's perspective: "I did this. Then I did that."*

The output:

> *Jon did this. Then Jon did that.*

Let's break it down. The key thing we want to do is "rewrite in 3rd person". The specifics are that we want the rewrite to be from Jon's perspective and the quoted text we want to rewrite.

Here's another prompt that I used for this book:

> *Describe an old mining town in the West Virginia mountains that's now a ghost town.*

Describe is the keyword. From there, I provide "what" I want the AI system to "describe": an old mining town. Then I provide more context to shape up the specific content I'll looking to build: in the West Virginia mountains that's now a ghost town.

5 Things to Try

Write a prompt to build a haiku about a tree

1. What do you want the AI to build = A haiku
2. What are the specifics = describe the tree
3. Any context you want to provide = where is the tree?
4. Example: Write a haiku about a red tree on a mountain

Take the haiku output from above and ask AI to rewrite it as a free-verse poem

1. What do you want the AI to build = A free-verse poem
2. What are the specifics = your poem
3. Any context you want to provide = add more information about the tree or environment
4. Example: Rewrite the following as a free-verse poem "poem content" where the tree is blooming.

Try to have AI describe a character from a story you're imagining

1. What do you want the AI to do = Describe a character
2. What are the specifics = talk about your character
3. Any context you want to provide = does the character have a tick or some identifying behavior?
4. Example: Describe a character who is a knight in the red army that constantly washes his hands

Describe a scene for your story

1. What do you want the AI to do = Describe the scene
2. What are the specifics = a steakhouse that serves salad
3. Any context you want to provide = what's something unusual about the scene
4. Example: Describe a steakhouse that serves salad with green walls and white floors.

Write some dialog for your characters using AI

1. What do you want the AI to do = Respond to character X
2. What are the specifics = what emotion do you want to have your character express
3. Any context you want to provide = is there something else going on outside of what is being said
4. Example: Respond to Jon with an angry response that hides embarrassment

Say what you want, say what you mean

I hope you enjoyed this exploration of Prompt Engineering. It will be a critical skill in the world of AI. Being able to ask for what you want and get it fast will be an important skill as more and more AI tools become part of our lives.

Remember, be clear on what you want, provide specifics and then layer in context as needed to get what you're looking for. Above all, experiment, explore and have fun.

Best of luck in your Prompts!

PRE-ORDER THE NEXT BOOK

The Treasure of Crumbling Caverns: Keymasters Book 2 is available for pre-order now!

Anna ventures deep into Mirror Mountain, but she doesn't go alone. Her and her stepmom, Naomi Dugan, must face monsters, traps and their own self-doubt as they navigate the Crumbling Caverns. In this trial, they must clear the path for the other trials to be completed by solving the Cavern's many strange puzzles. Along the way, they meet two strangers, one who will help them and one who will lead them astray. Can they figure out which is which and navigate the Caverns before time runs out?

Discover the next Keymaster adventure in:

Treasure of the Crumbling Caverns.

STAY CONNECTED

Hey, Tim here. I hope you enjoyed The Trial of Mirror Mountain. There's a lot more to come from Eric, Nico, Anna, and many of the other characters you met in this book, so stay connected to hear the latest news about the Keymaster Series.

You can keep up to date by following my website at:

https://timkulp.com/books/keymasters

Drop me a line there and let me know what you thought of the book.

Reviews

Please leave a review of the book on your favorite bookstore to help other readers find Trial of Mirror Mountain. Honest reviews are always appreciated.

OTHER BOOKS BY CY BORGMYN

CREDITS

Author: Cy Borgmyn (Tim Kulp)

Cover Design: Cy Borgmyn using MidJourney, Art Breeder, Daz3d, and Adobe Photoshop

Editors: Annie Cassidy, Linda Trout

General Font: Adobe Garamond Pro

Chapter Headings Font: Sophia CC

Illustrations: Cy Borgmyn using MidJourney, Adobe Photoshop, Daz3d, Real Allusion Character Builder, and Adobe Illustrator

Writing Software: Microsoft Word, Pro Writing Aid, Adobe InDesign

Special Thanks: Marlye, Becca, Micah, Linda, Maria. Thank you all for your comments, input and thoughts on the story.

Until next time...let the games begin.